DISC

The
TENDER
BIRDS

ALSO BY CAROLE GIANGRANDE

FICTION
All That Is Solid Melts into Air
Here Comes the Dreamer
Midsummer
A Gardener on the Moon
An Ordinary Star
A Forest Burning
Missing Persons

NON-FICTION
Down To Earth: The Crisis in Canadian Farming
*The Nuclear North: The People, The Regions and
 the Arms Race*

The
TENDER
BIRDS

a novel
Carole Giangrande

inanna poetry & fiction series

INANNA PUBLICATIONS AND EDUCATION INC.
TORONTO, CANADA

Canada Council Conseil des Arts
for the Arts du Canada

 ONTARIO ARTS COUNCIL
CONSEIL DES ARTS DE L'ONTARIO
an Ontario government agency
un organisme du gouvernement de l'Ontario

 Canadä

We gratefully acknowledge the support of the Canada Council for the Arts and the Ontario Arts Council for our publishing program. We also acknowledge the financial support of the Government of Canada through the Canada Book Fund.

Cover design: Val Fullard

The Tender Birds is a work of fiction. All the characters and situations portrayed in this book are fictitious and any resemblance to persons living or dead — with the exception of historical personages — is purely coincidental. Names and incidents are the products of the author's imagination and historical events are used fictitiously.

 MIX
Paper from
responsible sources
FSC
www.fsc.org FSC® C004071

Library and Archives Canada Cataloguing in Publication

Title: The tender birds : a novel / Carole Giangrande.
Names: Giangrande, Carole, 1945- author.
Series: Inanna poetry & fiction series.
Description: Series statement: Inanna poetry & fiction series
Identifiers: Canadiana (print) 20190147792 | Canadiana (ebook) 20190147806
| ISBN 9781771336659 (softcover) | ISBN 9781771336666 (epub) |
ISBN 9781771336673 (Kindle) | ISBN 9781771336680 (pdf)
Classification: LCC PS8563.I24 T46 2019 | DDC C813/.54—dc23

Printed and bound in Canada

Inanna Publications and Education Inc.
210 Founders College, York University
4700 Keele Street, Toronto, Ontario, Canada M3J 1P3
Telephone: (416) 736-5356 Fax: (416) 736-5765
Email: inanna.publications@inanna.ca Website: www.inanna.ca

For Brian

There is the heaven we enter
through its institutional grace
and there are the yellow finches bathing and singing
in the lowly puddle.

—Mary Oliver

Prologue

2001

MATTHEW REILLY'S RUNNING LATE. It's early morning, he's about to fly, his cab's waiting. Last night, he dreamt about Valerie. Glancing in the mirror, he smooths back his thinning hair before he heads out the rectory door. There's a chill in the air, autumn's coming, but the clear sky is indigo blue, edged with dawn. He notices a fading star or two, perhaps a planet. In his youth, when Valerie had been his lover, she'd taught him the names of a few bright stars. He wonders if she still recalls them. By the grace of the internet, she'd come back into his life again. Email, he thinks, is a blessing — it allows one to keep a distance. He'd have to remember to ask her about the stars.

In the cab, Matt recalls how he felt last night, busy to the point of desperation, knowing that what ailed him was an old dread, an unnameable fear of chaos made worse by exhaustion. Due for a vacation, he'd been packing for this early morning flight, a visit to his sister on the coast. In his carry-on: laptop, breviary, academic journal, cell phone. He'd set out his black slacks and short-sleeved shirt, his Roman collar for the morning. His identifying dress would get him good service in Boston, nods of respect at the airport, a quicker-than-average pass through security as they'd give him a look-see and find a decent, trustworthy man. *The body doesn't lie,* as they say.

Matt had a degree in psych, and he knew how they trained those guards. A screener would see a trim man with blond hair, blue eyes, a ruddy complexion, and a smile that was kind enough, though perhaps a shade cold. The metal detector would swipe his chest and shriek at a small silver crucifix on a chain. That would be it.

He packed a few pairs of running shorts and sweat socks. Exercise paid off — he looked good on TV. Yet when he'd watch his videos or DVDs, he was perceptive enough to notice a hardening of his expression, that dreaded priestly visage of youthfulness stiffening into old age without the ripeness of maturity. On the screen, he'd glimpsed a man who was absent from his longings.

Chastened by the thought, he paused from packing, took a deep breath, gripped his hands behind his head and stretched, feeling the pull of his muscles, trim against black shirt sleeves. At least he was presentable. He hadn't gorged on junk food at Parish Council meetings, and he didn't suffer with the lonely bottle that afflicted so many other priests. In his mid-fifties, he enjoyed good health.

Much in demand, he'd overloaded every circuit — books, articles, reviews, interviews, teaching, pastoral work. So much had been given to him, so little of it deserved, he thought. He should be generous; yes, yes to every request, his hand gripping the phone in a fury of muscular spasms. *Breathe*, he'd say to himself, directing his breath to release his hand. *Relax*.

He could have flown out to the coast that evening, but it was Monday, a teaching day, with office hours for graduate students who often came late. Traffic, they explained. If he'd turned them away, he'd be in L.A. by now. Yet he felt that life had been good to him and more than cruel to the drivers of Boston, with all the construction detours downtown, and the Central Artery backed up into the next life. It was no fault of theirs, being late. He knew of many worse sins.

Even though weary, Matt was still a hopeful man. In his faith, the world was a gift, a sign of grace, and all of creation was the echo of this mystery. His every action — the movement of his hands in folding a garment, the choice of a book to read on the flight — made visible the blessing of the unseen. He was packing for a spiritual journey, as if there were any other kind.

How would it be if I just went on vacation? he thought.

The phone rang. He let it ring through to his voice mail as he squeezed his running shoes into a pouch. *Done.* He zipped up the suitcase and shoved it into a corner. Then he sat down at his desk, hiding his face in his hands, pressing his fingers into his temples, as if to massage away an intensity of feeling, one that was unfamiliar and disquieting. For weeks, he'd been seized by the thought that he needed to leave his calling. He was too alone, afraid of spending his last years in a narrow, empty room, denied forever the intimacy that gives married people solace in their old age. Yet the layman's life appeared to be a jangle of distractions, a tiresome maze he'd have to learn to navigate. He'd never owned or rented a home, never shopped or cooked or taken his shirts to the cleaners. Unskilled in the tasks of ordinary life, he had no idea how he'd cope.

Matt hadn't been sleeping well. Before retiring, he'd pray Compline, the night prayer of the Church. *May the Almighty Lord grant us a peaceful night and a perfect end.* He had to rise early to catch his plane, but after an hour or two of fitful sleep, he woke up. Darkness slammed into him the way a twister hits the ground.

A soldier in a southeast Asian jungle — the image blurred in his memory like torrential rain on a windshield, the wipers going full tilt. Even now, there was only so much visibility. The rain had poured down, a monsoon, a howl of danger. He opened his breviary and prayed, *Oh God, save me, and by your mercy free me.* Yet his hands were chilled, as if they still held a rifle, and he felt an old madness, like a terrible thunderstorm battering the earth.

At times like this, he asked himself why he'd want to leave the priesthood, where he was safe. He feared the absence of prayer in his life, what the end of discipline might mean. He wondered if he hadn't prayed enough.

Matt stares out the taxi window. Irritated from lack of sleep, he's dreading this ride to the airport. Traffic tie-ups even before dawn — how inconvenient the city's become. Roadblocks and detours, the Big Dig like some monstrous worm grinding and tunnelling its way underground; hideous orange garbage trucks, their iron mandibles poised to crush cabs and bikes; the side streets plugged with FedEx deliveries and September's lineup of student moving vans. It's outrageous, he thinks — the jackhammering chaos of downtown Boston. When the cabbie asks "Where to?" he's about to say, *Where the hell do you think, at this hour?*

He catches his own reflection in the rear-view mirror, the white edge of his Roman collar.

"Logan," he says. "Terminal C."

Matt's driver is a brown-skinned man, his head covered by an embroidered cap. Nowadays, many of Boston's cab drivers appear to be Muslim, and he wonders how they juggle their fares to accommodate their religious practice of praying at regular hours. Thinking about these devout men brings solace on his rides to the airport. As he gazes out the window, he imagines a city full of reverent souls, hundreds of Muslim cabbies pulling up to the curbs on Tremont and Boylston, Charles and Beacon Streets, all of them unaware of irritated shoppers, women loaded with bags from Macy's and Filene's, trying in vain to hail off-duty cabs. Each man with a prayer rug under his arm is walking along the criss-crossed paths through the flower beds of the Public Garden and the Common, each prostrating himself by the fountains, or alongside the statue of George Washington or Charles Sumner; each man a compass-needle swinging eastward. Oblivious to staring tourists, bongo-drumming buskers, lunchtime strollers on their cellphones, the devout would send up their insistent murmur to heaven, that Allah most merciful might hear them.

Such faith, he thinks. He feels a twinge of sadness.

He pulls the breviary out of his computer bag, and in the dim light, he begins to read. *Oh God, come to my assistance. Oh Lord, make haste to help me.*

Matt has a fondness for cab drivers, whatever their faith and whatever the road conditions. He relies on them because he doesn't drive. As a youth in a New York City suburb, he suffered a blackout on the Tappan Zee Bridge. He was ill, his licence was revoked, and he's never tried to get it back because its loss taught him humility.

He's thinking this as his cab enters the tunnel, a tube of darkness lit by the headlights of oncoming traffic. His watch says seven-fifteen, Eastern Daylight Time. The plane is leaving in an hour, and nothing's moving. The long line of vehicles appears to congeal into a glistening gel squeezing its way out of the tube. It's getting late. He lets his mind idle, trying to imagine the French island of Saint Pierre where Valerie's gone to contemplate the flowers of a harsh terrain. Lacking more casual language, he'd told her he'd pray for the success of her retreat. He glances up. The cars ahead aren't moving.

"Rush hour," says the cabbie. "Volume of traffic."

"Is it always this bad?"

"Some days worse."

The cabbies always say that. The traffic starts moving again, and as soon as the cab emerges from the tunnel and into the light of day, Matt looks up at the cloudless sky and remembers a pious sister from grammar school who'd describe such blue as the sky of Mary, perfect and unsullied by the cloud of sin, an azure garment embracing the world. He finds this image saccharine, but he also finds it calming to imagine each morning as a new creation. In his heart, Matt has always thanked that sister, who'd done for him what he felt the Church did best — how it haunted reality with signs and symbols, with ghosted layers of meaning.

"What airline?" asks the cabbie.

"United."

The cab pulls up to the curb. There's construction at the airport, and in order to get to the check-in, he has to wheel his suitcase through a jerry-built entranceway of plastic sheeting and wooden planks, leading him to the escalator that descends into the main lounge. It's seven-forty — they start boarding his flight in five minutes. Below him, the check-in hall is jammed, and the passengers form a long, meandering sausage-link, its human casings stuffed and bulky with backpacks and carry-ons. He gets off the escalator and makes his way to the United Airlines check-in. There'll be a lineup; there always is. A passenger's holding things up, showing his passport. *Great moments in human stupidity,* Matt thinks. *It's probably expired.*

His turn. The agent glances at his ticket, stamps his boarding pass and looks at it with concern, with a deferential nod that frames her face in tight black curls. As she turns her eyes on him, he catches the gleam of a tiny gold cross around her neck. "You're running late, Father," she says. "Just go. I'll call and ask them to hold the plane." Matt hears a Spanish lilt in her voice. *What a little sweetheart,* he thinks.

This sort of thing happens so often that he accepts it as routine, at least in Boston. Grateful for the grip that the Hispanic church still has on its adherents, Matt hits the escalator two steps at a time, then dashes off to security. He shows his ID and boarding pass, then sees that one of the screening-posts has no guard. On other flights, he's noticed the lack of staff, along with a few harried passengers who'd slip through unchecked. He's tempted to do that today, and then he remembers that his Roman collar had attracted the ticket agent's notice. It could also be noticed by a guard. In any case, it would set a poor example if a priest took advantage.

"Over here," says the guard at the next post. There's a line ahead of Matt. He empties his pockets of keys and change and places them in the plastic box. He shoves his briefcase through the X-ray machine. As he walks through the metal detector, it squawks at the cross he wears under his shirt. "Sorry, Father," says the woman who runs the wand over his body. When he goes to the counter to claim his carry-on, the guard asks him to turn on the computer. Matt does, then glances again at his watch, an ancient one that belonged to his father. Patience and fortitude are gifts of the Holy Spirit, he thinks.

While his laptop boots up, he eyes the TV monitor overhead. A travel ad — the face of Big Ben, about to chime the hours over London. A mesmerizing sight, all Roman numerals and giant hands. He shoves the computer back in the bag.

Wonder if that little gal got through to the plane. The gate's up ahead. Matt's running.

Matthew

Why He Loved Birds

"I MISSED THAT PLANE," said Matt. "I don't know why God saved me." He did not think it appropriate to tell his parishioner that he had never offered comfort to Valerie, his love before entering the priesthood, the woman whose quiet retreat to a French island left her in anguish on a tragic day. She had lost her son to the plane he missed. It crashed into the tower where the young man worked. Ten years on, and he mentioned none of this.

"You know about...?" he asked.

"Everyone does," said Alison.

He felt embarrassed, having almost stumbled into an idiotic question, as if the woman before him had been cloistered on that tragic day, without TV or the internet.

"All of us were meant to die that day," she said. "Yet some of us lived. Who knows why?" She looked at him with a fearless seeing that went beyond sight. He felt her eyes capture him as a camera's shutter freezes time. Or as a hawk's eye holds its prey, with the same fierce, unguarded innocence. She had thick dark hair that she wore in a glistening braid, a pale face as calm and serene as moonlight. Saint Alison, he'd think sometimes, amused by her earnestness, but not prepared to dismiss it.

By her side was a cage containing a peregrine falcon, a fierce-looking creature that could neither hunt nor fly. Daisy was Alison's best friend, a peculiar companion, a proud species with a humble name. *Peregrine* for wanderer.

Her keeper had been sorting and boxing books in the library that served as his part-time office. The church was about to close; the books were to be sold. Alison was intrigued by the fact that some of the volumes excluded from the sale were falconry guides, attesting both to the Father's interest in the subject and to his failure to cloak the sport in any form of spiritual drapery. It was while she was putting these books aside that Matt told her the dreadful story of the plane he missed, and the terror of that day that had so injured humankind.

Alison had asked him an innocent question. She'd asked him why he loved birds.

"Because of a terrible thing that happened," he said. "Because I needed to love something."

Ten years earlier, he had supervised a doctoral student from Toronto whose mother owned a plant nursery. This fact, otherwise of no concern, piqued his interest since his old friend Valerie ran her own lawn and garden business. Mentioning her name, he learned from his student that Valerie's gardening truck was a familiar sight in her neighbourhood.

He thought no more of it until the attacks, when his student emailed him to let him know that Valerie Lefèvre had lost a son that day. He ought to write her a letter of condolence, he had thought at the time. He had her address; he'd sent her his books. Yet although they'd renewed their friendship, it was sustained by intellect and bounded by restraint. By unspoken agreement, they did not discuss her children or their names.

He had pulled out his scratch pad and began to draft a letter of condolence. *Dear Valerie, I am writing to express my sorrow at the passing of…*

He had torn the page off the pad, crumpled it up, and tossed it in the garbage. He had thought that the least he could do was send her a Mass card.

He did not have the name of the bereaved.

He'd had to give a homily that Sunday, words of comfort for a rattled congregation. Something about people who'd said their last "I love you" into their cellphones.

He had wondered if Valerie had received such a call.

Curious, Daisy gripped her perch, her talons like the curved tines of a sharp fork, her wide eyes dark at the centre, ringed with gold like two great suns in eclipse. Having settled into the large cage that Alison had placed in the corner, she eyed her keeper and the dark-suited man. She was restless, in need of a stretch, and so she stood tall, flexing her wings. They were an elegant falcon's wings, but awkward, unbalanced, injured in her fledgling days. A prideful rustle and flap were all she could manage, a short leap to a higher perch. She settled down again.

"Daisy, don't fuss," whispered Alison. She glanced at Matt. "Is it okay if I..."

"Sure," he said.

Alison slipped on her glove, opened the cage door, and enticed Daisy to her hand with a lifeless mouse that Alison dangled by the tail. Hope she didn't find that in the church, Matt thought, but the falcon, having managed awkward flight, snapped up the treat, arranged her wings, and settled down on Alison's gloved fist.

"There's a good girl," said Alison, and she kissed her head.

"It's safe to do that?" asked Matt.

"We're friends."

He sensed a trace of annoyance in her voice. As if I didn't know that, he thought.

"Daisy is from God," she said.

It wasn't the first time he'd heard her say this. She'd speak the words with such tender conviction that Matt felt churlish for doubting their truth. Yet she seemed strange, a pilgrim on a winding road, one either laced with mines or lit by the grace of God. He found her perplexing.

Alison was a spinning top, sending off sparks. Yet she was also feral, silent.

Daisy was as still as a fire about to start.

He wasn't sure what to make of the pair of them.

She was a helpful parishioner, a quiet participant in church activities, a veterinary technician in an animal hospital. She displayed her falcon in schools, wrote poetry, and volunteered to do odd jobs around the parish. More than that, she'd taken up sitting on park benches with Daisy, talking to homeless people about her fierce little friend, showing kindness to some of the same poor souls who drifted into Mass with occasional grunts and shouts and loud, off-key singing. People were drawn to her. She said little but listened with her whole body as if her nerves were woven of confessions and secrets, a nest for the nurturing of others, and not a body at all.

She insisted that the great birds were her calling.

Daisy was never far from her, an injured creature that she nursed back to health. A peregrine falcon, nonetheless; a bird of prey. There were times when he wondered about Alison's state of mind.

He sensed that she had not had an easy life, that she needed protection, as a daughter might. Unlike most parishioners and students, she did not tell family stories. Home had been Toronto, but her mother lived in Montreal. Somehow, she had ended up in Boston. Perhaps her wandering spirit made him feel, as many did, that he could talk to her, as if she would receive and absorb his words till they evaporated like a puddle of rain in brilliant light.

"I believe that Daisy is capable of love," said Alison.

"Well, who knows?"

"Would you like to hold her?"

Matt paused, transfixed by the wild creature. "I think for now that I should just ... contemplate her," he said.

"Yes, she puts me in awe," said Alison.

In few words, Matt told her that he had learned to enjoy birds, to see their great migrations as avatars of grace, as healing for a sky so wounded on that cruel September morning. He was not as adept as his younger friends at the skill of identifying them. He did his best, taking comfort in the beauty of their flight, in the goodness of creation.

Alison held Daisy and sat across from him, her posture erect, as statuesque as a dancer's, her gaze as primal as the bird's. He could feel her eyes as they traced the lines of sorrow etched into his skin. He felt certain that she must feel his words inside her, their frantic wing-like beating. He told her — with as much brevity as possible — that after the attacks, he felt as if he'd been given a second life, one he was unsure he deserved. He'd renewed his efforts to be a good pastoral psychologist, a professor who might offer insight into the world's calamities. He worked; he never stopped working. He wrote a book about recovering from grief, another about the relevance of the Cross in a time of sorrow and fear, another about blessing the stranger in our midst. He gave seminars and workshops on bereavement counselling, said two Masses at St. Bartholomew's on weekends because they were short of priests, spent some time in an online raptor chat room in Lower Manhattan because there were frightened, lonely people who needed the reassurance that they and the great hawks were held in the embrace of God. He also studied his *Field Guide to the Birds of North America*. He loved warblers, their springtime migration, their jewel-like beauty — their quick brush-strokes of colour and sunlight.

Alison listened, no doubt sensing what he'd left unsaid. She did not pry. He saw her eyes gazing at his hand, which rested over his heart as he spoke.

"This is close to your heart," she said.

He lowered his hand, embarrassed. He did not speak of his palpitations nor of his near breakdown and loss he suffered. "It is," he said. "True enough."

"You were blessed to miss that plane," she said.

"Sometimes we are blessed," he said, "at the expense of others."

"You came to this parish. It's a simple place. A retreat."

"And now it's closing."

"I've given up trying to understand the world," she continued. "I live with mystery enough." She glanced at Daisy as she turned her head in Matt's direction.

"Yes," he said. "I can see."

"The care of falcons is a spiritual practice. I can show you."

Matt thought about this. He had not found relief in telling his story because he had not told all of it. Yet he liked reading about falconry, its majestic creatures, its lost Eden of the soul. To win the trust of a bird of prey, it was necessary to be kind and patient, to cultivate an inner stillness, to become for the hawk a perch, a branch, its source of food and safety—its servant, not its friend.

He wanted to empty himself, to love, to be at peace. To live a life of service, not one of punishing exhaustion. "I am curious," he said, "about every spiritual practice."

She hesitated. "I can try to explain how it came to me. I can write things down."

Matt thanked her.

Moved by their encounter, Alison wrote a reflection — in her own mind, a prayer.

"Words are a gift from God," her email said.

The Mother Hawk's Soliloquy

IN OUR AERIE, *out of twigs and paper scraps, we have built the nest that is our home. One of us hunts. The other watches over our young. Both of us survey the grounds below — the fountain, the rooftops, the green leaves stirred by daybreak — all the places they will light upon when they are old enough to fly.*

With our talons, we open each ripe segment of the unfolding day; with our eyes, we uncover its dangerous beauty, offering safety while we can. Underneath me, my little ones shelter from the terrible strangeness of the world. Under my wing, they sleep.

Not long ago, they slid out of my body, encased in brittle shells, and I warmed them into life until I felt them stirring, drawing air, a sharp protrusion breaking through the frail crust that held them, their slight voices crying out for food. Then a beating of the air, the blue sky sliced by wings as their father returns, carrying prey for me to feed them. Small and brave and curious, the hatchlings nudge their way into place, taking the food that I put in their mouths.

Each day they grow. Feathers appear, stubs grow into wings. Each day, I look outward, and their eyes follow mine. Here you will fledge; there you will roost. See where I have hidden food; see where I perch in the rustle of green. Behold the frail earth below, the eggshell sky where no one is safe.

Matthew read her composition, then wrote an email. "Alison, you write with great empathy. You make God alive in our world of uncertainty and beauty. I will ponder these words. Blessings, Fr. Matt."

He read it over again to make sure it struck the right tone. Pastoral, but not too personal. Almost forty years a priest, he'd become adept at keeping his distance.

He hit, "Send."

Two Weeks Later Came Easter

MATT WAS NOT FEELING WELL, his body clouded with light-headedness, a trace of nausea. He had just finished celebrating the final Mass of the day, after which he greeted parishioners, grateful to return to the sacristy to remove his vestments. He wanted to go home, to lie down.

The eggshell sky where no one is safe.

He now understood that Alison did not feel safe, and why.

She must have gone to an earlier Mass, he thought. He'd been told that she was taking Daisy to an Easter Sunday raptor display at a local park, a family event. He felt certain that she was avoiding him. Just before Holy Week, she had come to his office to continue sorting and boxing books, and she learned, by accident, that the two of them had once met. It was a brief encounter. She had been desolate and wanted prayers. He had ignored her, conversing with a rather superficial young man who seemed far more aware of her than he did. He should have noticed her desperation. He should have helped her. He didn't.

Enough. He'd save it for another day when he was feeling better. Alison was upset and needed space; he understood that.

Alone in the sacristy, he took off his embroidered chasuble and was about to untie the cincture on the white robe underneath when a hard fist of pain crushed his chest, tore down his left arm, and knocked him to the ground.

A young woman in front of the church in Toronto, years ago. He doesn't know her name, but he knows it now. Her dark hair is spiked and erratic like a wild bird's crest, she is fading into the crowd, he cannot see her. All but the eyes — they burn with a sunlike fever. They ask him why he was living, why he will not acknowledge her. She reaches out to hand him something. "Prayers," she whispers, as she begins to vanish. All but the eyes, which said, "Save me."

The thought that ran through his mind: No one will save him.

Yet what of the red-tailed hawk in flight, looking for height and a place to roost. It's a female; she finds herself a crossbar on an old-fashioned telephone pole in a country outside of time. Soon, she accepts a mate, but there are no high trees for nesting. "Spring will find us a place," says the great hawk to her mate. "I will lay eggs and protect them; you will cover me with your wings."

"Pray for me, for the hawks carry our prayers to God," said Alison.

He watched the hawk, fierce and maternal, her wings brushing his face as his body drifts between the raptor and the world.

Before the priesthood, before the Vietnam war, he'd had a lover named Valerie. He ran away from her. He felt her absence in the fist of pain that grips his chest.

God save me, he prayed.

It was too much to ask God to spare his life again.

The sacristan found him, called 911.

I cannot ask God for my life back. The thought consumed him.

Pain knifed him, tore his chest open.

Other thoughts crowded in.

Gasoline from the plane, and then he caught fire.

Valerie's son, trapped in the building. How he must have died.
His son.
Another prayer. *God, take me now. I owe you a life.*
Matt is not sure what he sees in the doctors' eyes.
He thought of a young man, lost; of the plane he missed.
"My turn." He struggled to say the words out loud.
The absence of Valerie pierced his chest, his side.
Crucifixion story. Good thief, bad thief.
Roll of the dice. Could be either.

Electrodes on his chest, hooked up to a monitor, zigzag lines
telling the doctors what his injured muscle couldn't do. Blood
thinners, nitro, beta blockers. They'd given him an angiogram
to see how much damage had been done. Someone asked him,
"Have you any family members you could call?" He did not.
Both parents, dead of heart attacks. No siblings. His university
colleagues were busy. The pastor would come, Father Ron, a
kind-hearted man who was grateful for his help. "You'll be
here close to a week, Father," said the intern. "Someone will
have to take you home."

Matt had visitors in the hospital — parishioners from St.
Bartholomew's, colleagues from Boston College, in publishing
and media. Cameron Byrne came up from New York — his
theologian friend who could not have come here just to visit
him. In town for a lecture, he was sure. He asked Father Ron
to email his friend Elias — not to bother him, just to let him
know.

Except that Elias was at Mass that day. He'd been the first
to know.

Alison had not come.

"Family history?" his cardiologist asked. "Your father and
your mother both."

23

Pure DNA. What irony. Father Fitness, twice a week at the gym, stuck with clogged-up coronary arteries. He'd gotten the bad news a few years back. But he'd lost track of his meds in the crush of Easter. Parish life did that.

usmcHawkcam.ca

Natalie: Bad news, everyone, Great Speckled Bird had a heart attack. He's in Mass Gen Hospital.
Hawkette: You're kidding.
Falco: Don't get it. Told us he worked out.
BigBird: Poor GSB. Something must of got 2 him.
Downtown: U mean like stress.
BigBird: No, I mean like the Catholic Church.
Kestrella: Or bad genes.
Natalie: He collapsed after Mass. The sacristan found him.
Elias: We must go visit, Nat.
Downtown: Just never know, do you. Right out of the blue.
Falco: Hell, when your time's up, it's up.

When he was well enough, Matt opened his laptop and discovered an e-greeting card from his online friends. "Hope you're flying soon. Get well, Great Speckled Bird, from the Chatters," and they'd listed their silly nicknames: Hawkette, Downtown, Jumpflap, BluebirdofHappiness, Kestrella, BrightWings, Moby-Chick, BigBird, RatChow, ItsTimeToFly, Falco, Aero, Shalom, Peregrine (for Alison), Cameraman, a.k.a. Alison's new buddy, Cam, the theologian.

He read it over and over again. Their names no longer seemed silly. They read like an awkward incantation in a foreign tongue, a twenty-first century liturgy.

Kyrie Eleison. Lord, have mercy.
Everyone needs friends, he thought.

Shorehaven

IN MAY, WHEN MATT FELT BETTER, his superior decided that he should take a year's leave of absence from academic duties, posting him to a small parish on the ocean side of Cape Cod. It sat on Route 6 at the south end of Shorehaven, a weathered town of clapboard-fronted shops, its tiny streets clam-shacked and flower-basketed in summer, yet still a workaday place for trawlers and fishers' nets, for the dredging of clams and oysters. It had a small bayside beach popular with families, most of whom rented the cottages on its shore road. Matt was too exhausted to come up with a different plan, and so he gave up the urban comforts of the life he'd known.

He was fine with Shorehaven, its salt wind and spray, its changeable weather — the morning sky greyed out, as if it were a foggy window, later to be scrubbed clean by sunlight and the passing day. There he would live for a year in rest and retreat. He'd say Mass, spend time with parishioners, do cardiac rehab with a visiting nurse. He'd walk and read and pray and try to be open to the simple kindness of his neighbours. There were two light-filled rooms in the rectory set aside for him.

He was still in shock from the fact of his illness. Rest and pray, he thought, but I've never learned how to rest.

He remembered his breakdown after Vietnam and then he tried to forget it.

Our Lady of Mercy Church was a bland modern structure that, absent its steeple and cross, might have been mistaken by passing vacationers for a Holiday Inn. Matt didn't care what it looked like. He spent much of his time in the rectory, where a deck provided him with a quiet place to read and a view of the ocean in the distance. He did not want to mingle with vacationers, and having neither a car nor a licence, he had to rely on cabs or buses to get into town.

He soon met a parishioner who worked early hours on the docks. Since the birds were active and visible at dawn, he would sometimes ride into town with the man for a birding stroll on the bayside beach, then take a cab home. Afterwards, he'd celebrate Mass, assist with parish tasks, do some reading and gentle exercise, email his friends and colleagues. There were oceanside beaches close to the church, but Matt could not yet manage a steep climb — or even the stairs — across the dunes to the water's edge. He would build up his strength, he thought, for a hike that in his better days would not have taxed him at all.

From time to time, he logged on to the chat room, reassuring the hawk-nest watchers that he was well. He had other gentle distractions. In this tiny hamlet, there was a library, a summer theatre, even a bookstore. Parishioners introduced him to the town and often invited him to dinner. Yet for the most part, he kept to himself.

At the beginning of his stay, he'd received a get-well note from Alison, handwritten on stationery with a picture of a robin, its nest and eggs. "Dear Father Matt," she wrote. "I hope you are feeling better and that you will take as long as you need to get well.

"…As for me, I have been writing about my early life, allowing forgiveness some room to breathe."

She added that Daisy was doing well.

Matt emailed her, thanking her for her kindness. He had many such greetings from parishioners and friends, all of which he acknowledged with a simple sentence or two. It was a practised art, this type of response, couched in neutral language and signed with a blessing, one which, as a young priest, he'd learned from his superiors. He'd known by instinct that a priest must be judicious in his choice of words. He could not afford to have entanglements.

"How about just friends?" said Natalie, when he taught for a term in Toronto.

"I consider you my friends," he had replied, but he had meant it more for her husband Elias than for her. The pair were scholars, but Natalie was a wit as well, always laughing and talking, an uneasy eddy of anything-can-happen pooling around her.

Alison felt more like a daughter than a friend. He preferred that.

Perhaps he had no friends.

Matt also hoped to write. He'd withdrawn from texting, blogging, and tweeting as if he were peeling off layers of excess clothing, useless in the salt air, the scouring heat of summer. He wanted the world to forget about his former life.

Yet he didn't want to die. He knew what it might feel like to vanish.

What he wanted was to be bodiless. Pure mind.

At times, he could feel his decimation, cell by cell, as if he were starry matter in thrall to a powerful and massive darkness, a meticulous tugging and pulling apart of his self, gravity absorbing him, star by star. He let go of himself, gave into it, imagined his flesh as a kind of reverse Eucharist, consumed and eaten by the body of God.

Now, at night he would step outside on the rectory's deck,

gazing upward at the glittering sky. He'd pray for the grace
of dissolution. With joy, he'd feel himself about to disappear.
Perhaps he wanted to die, after all.
He would hear Alison's voice, a poem she wrote.

In the lifting of wings, wonder and sorrow both.
What flies, flies away from you.

By a Hidden Name

I first encountered Alison two years ago at a weekday Mass, shortly after I'd agreed to help out at St. Bart's. A stately young woman, she was as calm as early morning. She walked up the aisle, eyes straight ahead, purposeful, as if she'd come to meet someone, and then she took her seat. Throughout the Mass, she wore the same, intent look. From my vantage point on the altar, she never appeared distracted, as most people do at some point during the liturgy, a few of them dozing during the Eucharistic prayers (which, I have to admit, are both meandering and soporific). When she came up to receive Communion, I had the feeling that she was carrying something or someone. Had she lost a child, I wondered. Yet she did not appear either burdened or bereaved. It was as if she were dressed in solitude, a garment that fitted her well. She bore whatever it was with grace.

That evening, I turned on the local cable news station, watching with some amusement and frustration as the screen filled up with a jerky video sent in from someone's smart phone. Citizen journalists, newscasters called them, meaning they didn't get paid, a cheap way to fill in airtime. Then, all at once the sky went wild before my eyes.

A fledgling falcon, leaving its nest on the roof of the Hancock

31

Tower, its cloudlike reflections in blue glass, ideal for a young bird born for the sky, born to an instinct for immense speed and swift attack, yet unskilled in the symmetry of stealth flight; soaring, diving, unable to right itself from an impossible turn toward the Mass Pike to the south, spinning and crashing into a truck, bouncing off to the side of the road where an off-duty cop pulled over, saw the creature, put in a call to The Animal Rescue League, took out emergency gear in the trunk, and sped to the South Boston shelter.

The anchor's voice-over described the scene as the cop delivered the injured bird; then they cut away to the shelter's operating room. There was a vet in O.R. scrubs; working with her was a familiar soul with thick braided hair and contemplative gaze, the name tag "Alison" pinned to her blue smock. She was showing X-rays to her boss, who turned to the camera and spoke. "Looks like a broken femur and fractured humerus," the vet said. "A juvenile peregrine falcon. Likely her first time up in the air. Maybe her last."

Alison was prepping her for surgery. She touched the injured falcon, held it down, felt for its heartbeat through its thick cape of feathers, listened with the stethoscope, covered the bird's face with a mask and began to administer anaesthesia. Then I realized that she must have felt everything at once: the falcon's warmth, its fierce, unnameable strength, the poor creature's terror, not knowing what had happened, where it was.

Before it fell unconscious, the eyes of the peregrine falcon opened wide, and I felt certain that I saw what followed (I am, after all, a psychologist, a priest; surely I'd earned the right to intuition); that gazing into their wild innocence, Alison forgot herself, emptied her soul into the healing of its body, placed her hands upon its broken wing and prayed.

The Sunday following that television show, Matt had stood

by the church door, greeting parishioners. He said hello to Alison. "I saw you on TV," he told her, then asked her how the falcon was.

"She'll never be able to hunt in the wild," she'd said. "Her wings don't have proper symmetry."

Matt hadn't been sure what to say.

"If she's too much trouble, she'll be put down. I hope not."

"I'll pray for her," he said. "Does she have a name?"

"Daisy." Alison paused. "If she were banded, she'd have a code name."

"Daisy, the peregrine falcon." He frowned. He had tried to imagine adding the name to the chain of intentions he'd offer before Communion.

Remember, Lord, your people, especially those for whom we now pray, he'd thought.

For Daisy, the peregrine falcon.

Feathered fighter-jet. Natural-born killer.

Alison seemed to sense his disquiet. "By a hidden name, she is known to God," she'd said. "Don't worry about her name."

He had assured her that he'd keep both her and Daisy in his prayers.

She thanked him and left.

Although he enjoyed birds, he'd never before prayed for one. *No one has to know what you pray for. Only God.*

Matt recalled how Alison had looked in the video, her hand on the injured creature, feeling its warmth, its heartbeat, its utter strangeness.

Alison had been a regular Mass-goer, he wrote, *almost a daily communicant. You don't see that kind of thing in young people anymore. Given all the sex scandals in the Boston diocese, that's not surprising. And Alison's devotion made me feel somehow fraudulent, as if she were doing the Church an honour it didn't deserve. Yet she also made me realize that God had plucked each of us out of the muck of human trouble, had set us down, weeds and flowers alike in a giant vase, roses with dandelions and milkweed, each beholden to its own beauty and calling, and none of it about human ego, all of it a mystery. Her daily presence had been just that: ineffable, a gift unearned. Yet beneath the surface, I could sense an undertow, something not quite right with her.*

Some weeks later, Alison had sent him an email to which she'd attached a picture of Daisy. "She is progressing well in rehab. Thank you for your prayers."

He hadn't remembered to pray for the falcon.

God, he realized, had not been so negligent.

So that is when I began to sense what the great birds have to teach us, Matt wrote at Shorehaven. *But I cannot understand it. Since my heart attack, I am beginning to realize how limited I am, how mysterious everything is. So, I am trying to write, but I must admit that I do not open my heart with ease. Pausing to read over what I've written, I find my choice of words intriguing. Perhaps an illness of the heart should not have surprised me.*

Alone in Shorehaven, he prayed for Daisy. At that moment, he felt a terrible pang of loneliness, as if the act of supplication had erased the distance he'd placed between himself and his own humanity.

He *wanted* something.

He opened his laptop and began to write an email. "You have an extraordinary gift with animals," he wrote to Alison. "I regret that I did not acknowledge it sooner. I pray that both you and Daisy remain well."

He read what he had written. Too personal, he thought. He deleted it. Then, he wrote, "Blessings to you and your ministry with Daisy."

That, he thought, would be enough.

We Can Only Tell Stories

MATT WAS STUNNED BY ALISON'S RESPONSE to his email. "Dear Fr. Matt," she wrote. "I believe the care of Daisy to be my vocation. In my father's memory, I attend to her. I was only ten when we lost him. The attached may help you understand why this creature is so important in my life."

It touched him that Alison would entrust him with her thoughts. He had known so little about her.

Five years before I was born, my family left Boston for the lakeside city of Toronto, home of ravines and vanished rivers, of words spoken in a multitude of tongues, the first of which is silence. My parents never had much to say about that time, except that in his youth, my father refused a war, my mother concurred, and they preferred to live on the better side of a hopeless argument between young men and death.

Only my parents never mentioned that no one wins that argument.

My father Paul found a job teaching geography at the University of Toronto. Although well-liked by students, he was a quiet and solitary man, and apart from classes and academic meetings, he was just as happy to keep to himself. He was tall, fair-haired, and lanky, and his blue eyes crinkled — his whole face, in fact — whenever he looked upward, as if he were trying to glimpse some incredible brightness without doing harm to his vision. In his stance, his reserve, his comfort with the outdoors, he was a man you might have mistaken for a farmer. He kept a garden and enjoyed gazing at whatever bright stars might emerge in the dark of a city night.

Later, my dad told me that he was living in Boston when he took up the study of falconry. It made me think that Boston must be a special place, one that encouraged the love of animals and nature, and I asked my dad if we could visit the city, but he would only say, "We'll see." We never did go.

One day, I decided that when I grew up, I would look after sick animals, reclaim the place my father loved and live there on my own.

Mom and Dad bought a house on a shaded side street near St. Clair and Christie, one that meandered through a hilly west-end neighbourhood, alive with the seasonal commotion of migrating birds and playful squirrels, and there I walked through my childhood, hand in hand with my parents.

My dad would teach me about birds while my mother Jeannette photographed them. I was very small, and song-birds were my favourites — tiny, gemlike creatures, not the fearsome hawks and falcons that my father loved. I didn't tell him this, and besides, it didn't seem to matter at the age of six when everything is new, when so much happens for the first time.

Dad showed me the tracks of rabbits, the delicate imprints of sparrows and pigeons in the snow, the places where squirrels gathered their nuts for the winter. And when it snowed, I would fall into a state of awe and wonderment if a squirrel jumped, shaking snow from his branch all over me. I'd feel blessed at that moment, filled with a deep inner silence, as if we were in church, at Benediction. We were Catholics and everything felt holy, so as we walked together, I prayed for all the creatures in the wild.

As a child, I thought of God as most children do: as a giver of gifts, as the one who answers prayers.

I prayed for my mother. Dad took me to Sunday Mass, but Mom was often away on assignment and didn't go with us. When I asked Dad why, he said, "God is everywhere. She'll find him."

So, I thought at first that my mother was off on a special journey, looking for God. As a photojournalist, she worked with Lucien, a colleague from Radio-Canada. The two of them spoke French, and my dad did not, so she spoke to me, and I learned it with ease. It sounded like birdsong—its bright precision, its notes made of air.

My dad also said that you went to church for the comfort of praying with others. He had a young friend named Edward who sometimes joined us for Mass. He loved nature and was very kind to me, although he did not always seem happy, so I prayed for him, too.

Here is a prayer my father wrote: "Loving God, Tender Bird brooding on the world, protect us."

Matt went back and read what she wrote. "In his youth, my father refused a war."

He recalled that Alison had mentioned this a few months back, repeating things, as she often did: that her father had been a falconer, that he had to abandon the sport, preoccupied with fleeing to Canada, avoiding Vietnam. He saw now that the man had planted a seed of integrity in his daughter's soul. Schooled in her father's radical choice, Alison would feel empowered in her calling, however odd the tending of Daisy might look to others. Perhaps she wished to make this point, and that was why she'd sent him her reflections.

Had he stayed in Canada with Valerie, how different his own life might have been.

Matt wrote her back:

Alison, thank you for the kindness and trust you have shown me in letting me read your heartfelt reflection. So many of life's questions seem not to have answers. Perhaps we can only tell stories, as Jesus did. I also find writing a helpful spiritual practice.

I will say your father's prayer, and I will remember your intentions at Mass.

God bless you,

Fr. Matt.

Elias

TOUCHED BY ALISON'S WRITING, Matt used some of his time at Shorehaven to reflect on his deep connection with the city of her birth, with his own secrets that lay hidden there. In 2010, just over a year before his heart attack — and not long after Alison joined the parish — Matt had gone north to Toronto for a semester of teaching. A vanished summer echoed in the city's name, the place where he'd abandoned Valerie, but time had passed and life brought him now and again to the peaceful lakeside city for conferences and meetings of an academic nature, most of them connected to his writings on psychology and religion. He was to be a guest scholar and lecturer on Addiction and Spirituality — a new subject for the Catholic college on the east campus of the University of Toronto. He was looking forward to some time away from home.

Matt boarded a plane at Logan Airport, placing his foot with care upon the first step, then on the second, his movements slow, almost stately, as if he were celebrating Mass, his eye fixed on the acolyte carrying the cross ahead of him. A private liturgy. Each step in the ritual — the stamping of the ticket at check-in, the clearing of security, the showing of passports — contained within it a shadowy resonance, a prayer for the dead on the flight he'd missed so many years ago, a reminder of the life he'd been granted by running late that distant morning.

He'd never forgotten Valerie.

Then, a year after the catastrophe, when he finally wrote her an apologetic condolence letter, she sent him — without comment — a prayer card with the name of the child he'd fathered before he left for Vietnam, his dates of birth and death. By checking passenger lists, he learned that the plane he had missed was the same one that had crashed into the young man's building, setting a fire that killed him. Knowing these things, he had once thought of leaving the priesthood, then changed his mind, figuring he'd need the rest of his life to work this out, to read and write, to make his peace with the God of shadows.

He never spoke of this to anyone.

He did not like flying.

He thought of young Alison and her injured falcon.

Humans were never meant to fly, he thought.

He could feel himself falling into the cabin, zero gravity, sinking into his window seat. From his laptop case, he pulled out a book, tucked it into the pouch in front of him. *The Sacred Universe*. Years ago, he would have called it New-Age pap, authored by some frowzy feminist with braids and dream-catcher earrings. As if his own titles were any better: bestselling author of *The Wide Web of Grace* and *Click if You Feel the Spirit*. He cringed. Nowadays, he blogged and tweeted. He was a media go-to person for sturdy middle-of-the-road opinions on Catholic matters. Something of a celebrity for his academic work. Apart from that, he hadn't written a decent book in years.

At that moment, he looked up to see a tall man ambling down the aisle, glancing at his boarding pass, eyeing the empty seat beside him. Young, slender, chestnut skin, beard, dark eyes that seem to click on him — drag and click, as if he were a paragraph about to be deleted. The man had a duffel bag and a laptop case; a smart phone bulged out of his jeans pocket. On his red T-shirt was a large black vulture-like bird and something written in bold Arabic strokes.

Probably says, "Al-Qaeda Falconry Club," thought Matt. *Hope they shoved him through the baggage scanner. Headfirst.*

He took a deep breath, regretting how quick he was to judge.

His seatmate tossed his bag in the overhead bin, sat down beside him, and nodded hello. Matt acknowledged him, pulled out his book, and began to read. He sensed his neighbour watching him.

"Excuse me, I see you are reading *The Sacred Universe?*"

Matt's eyes widened. "Just a few chapters."

"I am a great admirer of Ms. Tucker and her papers on ecotheology. I am working on my thesis, also in ecotheology."

Sure called that one wrong, Matt thought.

The man's name was Elias. He was finishing his doctorate in Toronto, returning from a conference in Boston.

Matt explained that he was a priest, that he was on his way to teach at St. Michael's for the spring term.

"So, you are 'on loan.'"

"You could say that." Matt felt awkward, chastened by his snap judgment of his seatmate. "I see you like birds," he offered.

"Yes. Do you know there's a hawk's nest on campus?"

Matt said yes. He told Elias that the previous April, he'd spoken in New York at a colloquium on the intersection of theology and digital media, where he was introduced to a clutch of bird-nuts who connected every year to observe the spring migrations. Along with academic papers, they'd arrived with binoculars and field guide apps on their smart phones, thrilled that the conference was adjacent to a major migratory flyway. He joined them for an outing, invited by their conference host, the theologian Cameron Byrne — "Cameraman" to his Fordham students — lugging his video gear. That's when he learned that the hawk nestlings were a campus sensation at St. Mike's.

"A woman theologian told me all about it," added Matt.

"Oh?"

"Her name escapes me. Red hair."

Elias smiled. "We will show you the nest," he said.

Matt glanced at Elias' T-shirt.

"Are you a falconer?"

"My grandfather was. In Dubai. He sent me this as a gift."

Elias told him he was from Nigeria. The bird, he explained, was an African hawk-eagle.

"And what does the Arabic say?"

He smiled. "I believe they are words in praise of God."

They hit a patch of turbulence. Elias glanced at Matt, saw his pale face become strained and apprehensive. "I'm not much of a flyer," said Matt.

"In fifteen minutes, we will land," Elias said.

He saw Matt white-knuckle the armrest, then relax, open his breviary and glance at a prayer card. *In loving memory ...* it read. He caught the name: *Andre.*

Matt put the card away.

Pairs

MATT ENJOYED THE QUIET OF ST. MIKE'S. He liked the way the downtown campus seemed to absorb sound, to draw the clamour of the city into itself, moulding and shaping its hard edges into winter, as if the snow were some kind of primal fact, not to be dislodged from its place by mere human intent. Perhaps another word for this was death, but he wasn't sure. In any case, he found it both bracing and a comfort. In its demand for rigour, it seemed to embrace the life of study.

Yet upon his arrival, he'd looked forward to seeing the hawk's nest, to spending time in the calming presence of Elias and the quiet cadence of his words. Up ahead, he saw him standing in front of the library on St. Joseph Street. Next to him, swaddled in scarves and a parka, stood a tall woman, strands of russet hair curling around a finger of wind.

"I believe you have both met," said Elias.

That woman from the conference in New York. She had large blue eyes and fair hair alight with fiery undertones of red, what they used to call "strawberry blonde" in his youth.

There used to be a cat in the rectory with fur like that.

Natalie the theologian. Thesis on women in early liturgical practice. He had not made the connection earlier, that she and Elias were a pair. "I hope our group can go birding again in the spring," she said.

Matt assured her that it would be a fine idea.

"Now we are going to show you the hawks' nest," said Elias. "They like to perch on the cross at St. Basil's," said Natalie. "They've made a mess on the roof there, but it's steep, and poop runs off in the snow."

Matt said nothing.

"Brennan Hall's much worse," she continued. "The poop just kind of runs down the wall there and sticks."

Matt had no idea how to respond.

Silence.

She was digging a conversational pit for herself and filling it up with hawk poop. He felt sure that silence made her nervous. They walked along the north side of St. Joseph Street, past academic buildings, along a laneway edged by bare trees and genteel Victorian houses, places where you'd expect a more delicate sort of bird to dwell. At the head of the lane stood Brennan Hall — a grey stone Gothic Revival structure, approached by a flight of stairs leading to a flat-roofed entranceway thrust out from the building, framed on three sides by lancet windows.

"Now, Father, look up at that roof," said Elias.

Matt couldn't miss it. Within the Gothic elegance was a snarled mass of twigs, plastic bags, cords, newspaper, and string. There was a trace of white, calcified poop dribbling down the roof's facade.

"That's known as "slice," I believe," said Matt.

"The hawk poop?" asked Natalie.

"In falconer's parlance, yes."

"Guess I should use more precise terminology," said Natalie.

"Only if you're writing a thesis on the subject," said Elias.

Natalie laughed. Matt said nothing.

Elias explained that the hawk pair had arrived early last winter. During the study break before spring finals, the students relaxed by climbing up on the rooftops of adjacent buildings with smart phones and telephoto lenses to spy on the hawks and their hatchlings. *The Toronto Star* paid a visit and ran a photo feature on their website.

While he spoke, Natalie appeared transfixed. She gazed above St. Basil's Church, her arms lifting upwards, outstretched, as if she might float away. The air went silent. A pair of red-tailed hawks circled above her, then came to land on the church steeple cross, on either side of its horizontal bar.

"There go Armande and Josephine," said Natalie.

"You've found time in your busy life to name them," said Matt.

Natalie looked irritated. "Bishop Armande de Charbonnel founded St. Mike's," she said. "Josephine is for the Sisters of St. Joseph. They taught the first women students. We've named the hawks in their honour."

"They would look down and smile, yes?" asked Elias.

Matt acknowledged that they might be pleased.

"In spring, maybe you will bless the nest."

Matt said yes, of course he would.

He asked Elias about his thesis work, and their conversation drifted away from the nest and to scholarly matters. They enjoyed a pleasant stroll, and then Matt realized that Natalie was no longer with them.

"Natalie has gone to a meeting," said Elias.

"I see."

"You did not hear her say goodbye to you?"

Tattered Flag

IN SHOREHAVEN, MATT REFLECTED on his scholarly life, his occasional coldness and indifference — humbled by the fact that it was his heart and not his mind that had given out. That day at St. Mike's, he was astute enough to know he had annoyed Natalie, and yet he hadn't a clue how to respond to her lighthearted banter. It was a fact that apart from students and doctoral candidates — or the occasional parishioner — he had almost no contact with women. Although he socialized in Boston, he just wasn't comfortable wandering down the uncharted byways of small talk and chit-chat as a change of pace from serious conversation. He had no women peers, none he had chosen as friends. While in Toronto, he'd tried to work on this. He was trained as a psychologist, after all. He'd made Natalie nervous. He resolved to say *something* when she talked to him.

Nothing was simple. Matt had taken up birding in the hope of his soul's return to innocence, to a less self-conscious joy. That hadn't happened, not yet. At St. Mike's, he'd at least made an effort. Most days, he'd walk east of the nest at Brennan Hall, training his binoculars on the skies around St. Basil's Church, now and again spotting the hawk pair, then glancing upward at the steeple, at its crucifix. It's rather ordinary, he'd think, his eye passing through its slender form to the openness of sky. Whoever designed it must have understood that the faithful were meant to look beyond the cross, to understand that death is not the final story.

He hoped so. Every day something taxed him, wore him down with a sense of inadequacy. Having tried to be faithful, he felt as he grew older that his faith had become a tattered flag of victory, a hard-won banner planted on his barricaded life. He'd thought of leaving the priesthood a decade ago, then realized he could not. He hadn't the character, the strength to make a change. He was in his sixties now. Never mind — faith didn't depend on him for truth. Armande and Josephine, innocent creatures, could already sense that death was not the end. They loved this cross and would pay lasting tribute to their celibate namesakes as they incubated each brood of eggs and taught their young to fly.

They took such delight in life, these hawks.

So, to all appearances, did Natalie and Elias. He recalled that they'd given him a flyer with information on the hawks and a web link. The flyer explained that the previous winter, the two raptors mated on the crossbar, in a spectacular display of flapping wings and red tail feathers fanning outward. They did it more than once.

A photo showed the feathered pair, perched on the cross. Students had dubbed it, "The copulation station."

On Earth As It Is

ONE DAY, SOON AFTER HE ARRIVED in Toronto, Matt went into St. Basil's Church, sat in one of the pews, and dozed off.

Dreaming, his hands remembered a delicate bird emerging from the thin layers of white pine, the bird he'd coaxed from the wood, whittled, and given to Valerie who brought her guitar, her singing voice, into his backyard forest. He was going to marry her. He took her in his arms, and he was happy.

He woke up remembering that he had been afraid to love.

"I've been drafted," he'd told her, "and it's a rotten world, babe."

Bombings, wars, hijackings.

"My father had his war. Now I've got mine."

He had been wrong to turn his back on love. With the belated wisdom of the old, he now understood that the tormented world of his youth was the world as it is, and it would not change; that love was its only light, its candle in darkness.

And who do I love? he wondered.

He dried his eyes, knelt down, said a prayer for mercy.

In time, he had realized his call to the priesthood. God had shown him mercy, had he not?

Really, I have to shake off this mood. I just have to learn from this.

Matt got up, strode out of church, and left for the campus gym.

Men's Room

AFTER HIS HEART ATTACK, Matt grew thin, his body a fine sieve through which passed the dross of life experience, leaving behind a few bright glints of language. One term in Toronto, and a year later, recovering from his illness, he could retrieve very little about the courses he'd taught, apart from the notes in his computer. He felt as if parts of him were crumbling like a chipped vessel of sun-baked clay, and that he should submit to this process of erosion. Worse, he was beginning to acknowledge the years in which he'd existed in a kind of chronic pain, one to which he'd grown accustomed, as if his soul had become arthritic with the habits of priestly life.

You're tired, he thought. *You haven't been well, that's all.*

In Shorehaven, he felt consoled by the beauties of nature, the tattered ocean breakers, foraging ospreys, gusts of wind, and coruscating starlight.

He feared that so much of his life had been illusion.

He remembered how he'd felt those few months in Toronto. Happy enough yet restless, as if once again, he wasn't sure what he was doing with his priestly life. He liked the courses he was teaching, liked the idea of lending his name and reputation to a new program, but at the same time, he felt that the edge had gone from his lectures. Close to retirement age, he sensed that his life in the classroom was coming to an end.

Then there was the day when Gavin Moore strode into his

office and didn't bother to knock. Matt had been working on his laptop, updating his lecture notes. He jumped, knocking over a stack of papers.

"Oh, my God, I'm so sorry," said the young man. "I thought this was the men's room."

"All the more reason to knock," said Matt.

He bent over to retrieve the papers while the young man stood, perplexed, confused, his burst of energy ebbing away like a battery drained of its juice. He doesn't look well, Matt thought. *If he came with a cord, I'd have to plug him in.*

"I'm sorry," said the man. "I don't know what I was thinking."

Concerned, Matt asked him his name.

"Gavin Moore. I'm so sorry."

"Sit down, Gavin." Matt knew the name and felt his presence to be worrisome. The man was not a student. He was well-known to many in Toronto, including the police. Yet out of gratitude for his son's decision to reform his life, Gavin's father had funded the Institute for Pastoral Psychology, which had brought Matt to the college. The elder Moore was a prominent Catholic lawyer whose son had done time for drug dealing (one-year suspended sentence and a fine), then wriggled out of charges of living off the avails of prostitution (he didn't need the money and none of the women would testify). Afterwards, he wrote a book that became *Streetwise*, a recent bestseller describing his fall from grace and change of heart.

Matt asked him what he was doing on campus.

Gavin apologized again. "I am somewhat socially inept," he said. "You know, I got into trouble…"

"Yes, I know."

"I remember you, Father Matt. I met you in front of the church a few years back."

Matt could not recall him, or which church he meant; there were more than a few in his life.

"You and my dad — that was before I — anyway, your books changed everything for me. So, I thought I would say thanks."

Matt felt perplexed by the gap between praise and its ham-handed delivery. He eyed the man. "Did you really think this was the men's room?"

"I was daydreaming. I just ... lose track of where I am sometimes."

Matt asked him if he'd had any counselling.

"Some," he said. "I go to Mass, too. It helps."

Remembering the pitfalls of his own youth, Matt was struck by Gavin's odd mix of confusion, shyness, and bad manners. There was something guileless about the man, so impeccably groomed and dressed. He was privileged yet unable to read the usual signals sent by the world — its closed doors and appointment hours, the boundaries and courtesies of the everyday. It was out of concern, Matt thought, that he felt compelled to talk to him.

He asked Gavin what he was doing with himself, and he learned that he was preparing for a talk and book-signing on campus. Matt told Gavin that he would come. He looked hard at the young man. "If you need help," he said, "it's one of the things I do."

"You're very kind," said Gavin.

Matt gave him his card. "By appointment only," he said. "Call first."

Gavin glanced at the bold print: *Pastoral Psychologist*. He did not return Matt's smile. He slipped the card into his back pocket.

Caked Mud

MATT DID NOT WANT TO REMEMBER this incident with Gavin Moore. With the passing of time, it turned out that Natalie and Elias, untrained in psychology, had seen right through the man, while he, with his doctorate in pastoral psych, had flunked Gut Feeling 101. He'd viewed Gavin as a potential client, a mixed-up kid, someone he might counsel. Not a criminal.

He'd asked his friends if they'd like to come to Gavin's lecture.

"No, thank you," said Natalie. "What a disgrace. Rich dad — big fat thumb on the scales of justice."

"Are you sure about that?" asked Matt.

"One-year suspended sentence? Bought and paid for."

Matt said that prison was no place for him, that Gavin needed help. He told them the story of his impromptu visit. "I guess I'm inclined to forgive him and hope for the best," he said.

"Father, you have too kind a heart," said Elias.

"It just doesn't help to..."

"You should have asked about the girls he messed with," said Natalie. "If they'll forgive him."

"None of the girls spoke up," said Matt.

"None of them wanted a grilling in court."

"Yes, well, that often happens."

In retrospect, the memory of Gavin Moore's talk made Matt uneasy. He drew a crowd to the lounge at Elmsley Hall, since

53

faculty and students in the program knew of his relationship to their benefactor and felt obliged to attend. Matt thought that Natalie and Elias had chosen well by staying home. Gavin's talk combined a weird boyish charm with a cascade of platitudes about healing, openness, inclusivity, compassion, and community. There were also elements of self-justification — sexual incidents couched in euphemistic language, as if he were mindful of the sympathies of liberal priests and feminist nuns. What he offered instead was vacuous, as if crime and prison had been hosed away like dirt and grime from a child's boots. In the question-and-answer session, he offered little more than boyish innocence, as if life had left no mark whatsoever, as if the act of speaking and writing had cleansed him of memory itself.

A blessing, I suppose, thought Matt. *That must have worked well in court.* Yet it troubled him. Students were heard to murmur, "Is he for real?" Few of his books were sold and the crowd ebbed away.

Gavin gave Matt a signed copy of his book. Hoping that the young author might one day connect with the caked mud he'd tracked through his life, Matt reminded him to keep in touch. Gavin eyed him, dropped his voice. "If I need a shrink," he said, "it won't be you."

Matt was puzzled.

"I guess you don't remember me," said Gavin.

Matt wondered how he might have known him, hoping to God he hadn't heard his confession. It was not a thing he would have recalled, since until recent times, confessionals were booths where the penitent could hide his face.

Don't worry, he told himself. He could be lying.

"I don't remember you," said Matt.

"No?"

"We make it our business to let go of things," said Matt.

"I'm sorry," said Gavin. "I should not have said that."
"Find yourself some help, Gavin."
"You were very kind to me," he said.

Perhaps

LATER, MATT TOLD NATALIE AND ELIAS that he understood their reservations about Gavin, that not having been in Toronto when his case was in the news, he'd had little sense of what the fuss was about. He then told them for the first time that he'd had his share of troubles as a youth; no tangles with the law, but enough to warrant help from a compassionate priest who'd inspired him to find his calling. "I'm inclined to want to help Gavin, if I can," he told them. He wanted to add, "Before he does anything he shouldn't," but he didn't.

During his term in Toronto, Matt did not hear from Gavin again, but he read his book and felt unnerved by it, convinced that much of it was fiction, a fabricated change of heart, a calculated scheme to salvage his family's reputation. No, he thought, it's just mediocre writing by a man with a prominent name in this city. *Even so, some parishioners back home might learn from it.* He would occasionally see Gavin strolling across campus, then meandering along the paths in the quad, as if he had time on his hands. Sometimes, he came to St. Basil's for the noon Mass, where he'd sit in the back and check his email during the Eucharistic prayers, shutting down his phone in time for Communion. Matt wondered if he had a girlfriend. He felt certain that Gavin was not pondering a call to the priesthood. He seemed too charming, smooth, and untroubled. He would have liked to have spoken to the man, to listen to his story of survival, provided he had one other than the fiction he suspected him of writing. Perhaps Gavin was a psychopath. Whatever he was, Matt wished he'd disappear.

Gavin soon vanished from campus, evaporating in increments, like a dirty snowdrift in April.

Loneliness

MATT WOULD HAVE PREFERRED REAL FRIENDS in Toronto. He'd
enjoyed the company of Elias, who was himself reserved, a quiet
presence. In his residence, he'd chat from time to time with
Father Giles, an older priest from Paris who taught Theological
French, who spoke good English, but spent much of his spare
time watching French TV.

He knew himself to be shy. Yet in spite of loneliness, he felt
it a paradox that he was at home with solitude.

He enjoyed watching the great hawks flying over the campus
quad.

He did not enjoy reading email from people he would never
meet.

On one occasion, he was about to hit "Delete" when he
stopped at a fundraising pitch for the South Boston Animal
Shelter. He didn't donate. Instead, he clicked on "Our Pa-
tients" and opened a video showing Daisy, the injured falcon
and Alison, wearing her blue smock and name tag. She was
describing the creature's progress toward health, showing off
her large enclosure, her perch, water, and food supply. "She'll
never fly properly," said Alison. "She can make it up to the
perch, maybe fly to your glove, and that's about it. But Daisy
has a kindly temperament. Schoolchildren would love her."
She then invited online viewers to contact her at the shelter if
they'd like to have Daisy visit their school.

Daisy, he had to admit, was a fine-looking specimen.

Alone in his room, he shut off his laptop, bowed his head, and at last remembered to pray for the falcon and her keeper.

Big Birds, Big Brains

ON REFLECTION, THAT DAY CHANGED EVERYTHING. Maybe it had something to do with praying for Alison; maybe her appearance online was a prayerful visitation, a reminder from Daisy that only those who become as little children would inherit the Kingdom. He'd left his office and was striding across the quad toward Brennan Hall, when he glanced up at the nest. Armande had just made a floppy landing, the fan of his red tail snapping shut, his talons gripping a wad of pages from the subway Metro paper.

Keeping up on the news, thought Matt. He greeted Natalie, who was standing at the base of the building, staring upward.

"Reading matter," she said. "So Josephine won't get bored while she's laying eggs."

"Nesting materials, I would think," he said.

"Naw. She likes the crossword puzzle."

Natalie went on to tell Matt that last year, when she spotted eggs in the Brennan Hall nest, she contacted a reporter friend who worked for the *Star*. The woman arrived with a videographer, and they posted the nest and its brood of chicks on the newspaper's website. They got so many hits that the paper offered to sponsor a live-streaming webcam of the nest, along with a chat room. It would start this spring; the college loved the idea.

"Wait'll they hatch," said Natalie. "It'll be April. Exam week.

Students going nuts." She turned to him. "Matt, give this some thought. Think about getting involved. It's anonymous."

"And we'd discuss...?"

"Bird poop. And bird sex."

Matt smiled. "A limited field of inquiry," he said.

"We have to broaden the topic," said Natalie. "Which is where we come in."

She explained that the site needed knowledgeable moderators to provoke smart conversation and answer questions about hawks, so she'd pitched the idea to Elias and to Cameron Byrne at Fordham. Both were on board.

"Big birds, big brains," she said. "You could do it."

It would be the only chat room on the planet moderated by bird-watching theologians. Matt thought the whole idea was nutty, except for the fact that he knew Cameron Byrne, noted scholar and author of *Earth and Cosmos*, not some lightweight easy to dismiss. Nor could he discount Elias, a rational, well-spoken academic.

"I'll see what I can do," said Matt.

"Don't *do* anything," she said. "We thought it might be fun, that's all."

Gentle Soul

MATT GAVE IT SOME THOUGHT, then decided he'd give the chat room a try. As he got to know Natalie better, he began to feel more comfortable with her informality, more at home with her and Elias. It turned out that Natalie was an excellent cook. When Matt wondered where she found the time, Elias told him that she took after her foodie uncle — her hair, like his, the colour of a dazzling sunrise: *red sky at morning, sailors take warning.*

He wondered about this man who taught her to make crêpes, soufflés, and bouillabaisse — her mom's brother, both devout and probably gay, from the sound of it. "The family speaks of how he offered grace and blessed their food," said Elias, but Matt sensed a reason why the man was absent from their conversation, and he did not press Natalie for details. It was as if one day the man had dissolved, having kneaded his goodness into the fine grain of home-baked bread, having harvested life in the grape of a full-bodied Zinfandel.

Matt imagined that Natalie would forever be nourished by the memory of her uncle, holding this gentle soul in the breaking of bread and the blessing of wine, sure that God — if not the likes of Father Matt — might look upon the man with kindness.

FYI

To: Alison@sbas.com
From: FrMatt@utoronto.ca
Re: hawks' nest
March 15, 2010

Alison,
This may interest you. We have a hawks' nest at the college, and there will be a webcam and chat room. Log on at usmcHawkcam. ca. Blessings to Daisy.
Fr. Matt

Chat Room

SPRING CAME.

Natalie: Good morning, all.

Hawkette: Hello from Cape Breton!

Natalie: Hi from Toronto. I'm one of your moderators.

Cameraman: NYC here. I'm a mod, too. Welcome, guys.

Skywatcher: I'm all over.

Hawkette: Where's all over?

Skywatcher: Home's Indiana, but I'm in Afghanistan.

Hawkette: And they let you goof off online?

Skywatcher: Stress-buster.

Cameraman: You keep safe now.

Alison: I'm from Toronto, living in Boston.

Cameraman: Watcha doing in Beantown?

Alison: I'm a veterinary tech at an animal shelter. I'm fostering a falcon.

Cameraman: No kidding!

Alison: She hurt her wing and can't fly anymore. I'm going to take her into schools.

Cameraman: Kids'll go nuts.

Alison: Daisy's a good girl. She's OK with it.

Don River: I used to know a girl named Alison.

Alison: ?

Don River: Hot stuff. Good in bed.

......

Cameraman: Knock it off, Don. We're pulling the plug on you.

......

Don River: You can run, but you can't hide. Bye-bye.

Natalie: Just what we need on Day One.

Kestrella: How do you stop a creep like that?

Natalie: Pull their account. Trolls'll get us kicked off the website.

Cameraman: Alison? You here?

Natalie: Gone. Let's hope she'll be back.

Hawkette: So OK, deep breath. What do you do, Cam?

Cameraman: Shoot birds with a camera. Teach during the day.

Kestrella: Ornithology?

Cameraman: Environment. New branch of theology.

Kestrella: I do vid. Local TV docs in NYC.

Skywatcher: I do hawk patrol. :)

Natalie: Alison, if you're still here, it's safe now. We're all gonna be nice, right?

Kestrella: Chirp, chirp!

Cameraman: Kreeee! That's hawk for You Got It. You guys are too young to have heard of Jackie Gleason.

Hawkette: Whoozat?

Cameraman: TV personality from the fifties. He'd look over the audience and say: "You're a goooooooooood group!!!" Ditto for youze guys.

Kestrella: Hey neat! You speak Bronx.

Cameraman: Born in the borough. Got a nine o'clock class tomorrow. Gotta sign off.

A thousand people crashed the site on Day One.

"If you ever need a job..." said the *Star* reporter to Natalie.

"You'd hire a theologian?"

"I'm thinking you could blog about birds," she said. "Just in case the God thing doesn't work out."

Lurker

THERE WAS NO RECORD of the dialogue in the chat room; Matt only made note of what he recalled of its rapid back and forth — in his view, verbal birdseed flung on the ground and pounced on by pigeons or their human equivalent. He followed the rapid postings and observed the interactions. Snappy wit, and that one distressing interruption during the first chat, most of which he did not include in his notes. He wasn't used to the vile side of the internet, and more to the point, he was convinced that Alison wasn't, either. It was at his invitation that she joined the chat, so he felt he ought to be protecting her. But how, he wondered.

At least he could offer kindness, a reassuring presence.

Don River. What a weird nickname. At least it suggested a Toronto person, no one who would track her down in Boston.

Yet Alison had mentioned where she lived.

He hadn't yet joined the chat room, yet he couldn't shake the sense that Alison might be in danger, that someone might be stalking her. It didn't help that she came wrapped in innocence, swaddled in it like a newborn. A predator would find that enticing. Worse, she didn't protect herself, didn't use an alias. She drifted inside her own cloud, indifferent to the online convention. Clear as glass, she allowed others to peer inside her, no doubt secure in the knowledge that few could decipher what they saw. Perhaps in the end, that was her best protection.

Remembering Natalie's invitation, he decided to join the group so that he might look out for Alison. He began to search for an alias, something obscure and biblical. He pulled out his study Bible and started noting avian references. He began with the Book of Revelation.

"Has not my inheritance become to me like a <u>speckled bird</u> of prey that other birds of prey surround and attack? Go and gather all the wild beasts; bring them to devour." Jeremiah, 12:9.

He underscored the words.

From: FrMatt@utoronto.ca
To: Alison@sbas.com
Re: hawk's nest
March 18, 2010

Alison, I am so sorry about what happened to you during the first chat, especially since I encouraged you to join the group. I'm about to become a moderator, and I'd like to assure you that should you join us again, you'll be safe with three of us in charge. What you must do is to give yourself an alias. You need to protect yourself. You remain in my prayers.
Fr. Matt

Custody of the Eyes

APART FROM MATT'S CONCERNS about the chat room, the nest was alive with a new and mysterious kind of life, one that touched everyone, delighting the students and gracing his own table with improbable conversation. "We have permission," said Elias one evening over dinner, "if you would like to bless the nest."

Matt paused. "My pleasure," he said.

"The *Star* will cover it for sure," said Natalie.

"They've probably noticed that Armande is lining his nest with the *Star*," said Matt.

They hoped it could be in early April, before the eggs hatched. Matt felt touched. "I've never blessed a nest before," he said.

"We don't know anyone who has," said Elias.

Matt laughed, helped himself to seconds of *poulet aux pruneaux*.

"You're a fine cook," he told Natalie. "Michelin Three-Star: Exceptional."

Natalie thanked him. Opening her notepad, she began to list the possible order of the day's events.

She doesn't dwell on compliments, thought Matt. Strange, the look on her face, as if his compliment had scalded her, as if she'd touched a hot saucepan, then dropped it into the sink, a sizzle of cold water dousing her words. *Don't be ridiculous. She's modest, that's all.*

Although most times, Natalie was anything but shy.

He glanced at a photo on a table; teenage Natalie chopping veggies alongside a red-headed man who resembled her. Another photo showed the same man, his arm around a buddy.

That must be her uncle. The chef Elias said she resembled in looks and culinary skills. Yet he had the old priestly habit: *custody of the eyes, mind your own business.* Natalie drew silence around herself, as if she were pulling a drape around a hospital bed. She was in no hurry to reveal who she was. As if she were carrying something, a wound she didn't want known.

Like a Pilgrim

From: Alison@sbas.com
To: FrMatt@utoronto.ca
Re: chat room
March 18, 2010

Hello, Fr. Matt, thank you for your encouragement. I'm going to wait a bit before trying the chat again. That troll gave me a scare, as if he were lying in wait. It felt personal. It was my own fault for not using an alias. Here is my new one (hint – one word — like a pilgrim), so you can know it's me when I log on. As a rule, I enjoy online chatting. I offer prayers with Daisy, and I've never been bothered on Twitter.
Best wishes,
Alison

You've never been bothered on Twitter because your obsession with Daisy makes you look a bit odd, Matt thought. Yet Alison was young, nimble with language, skilled at the digital life in a way that he was not. He felt certain that with her avian training, she'd be an asset to the chat room, that she'd soon be back. He was the outsider. He didn't get the rambunctious chat, the website ticker that rolled up past a thousand on the first day, the students who chronicled these events in a blog called *Egg Roll* (where did they find time?), the daily updates on the *Star* online. More within his grasp were the students clumping around the steps in front of Brennan Hall, congregating along the lane running south from Brennan Hall to St. Joseph Street, smart phones and binoculars in hand.

Even so, he found the whole thing remarkable.

"Because the Holy Ghost over the bent/ World broods, with warm breast and with ah! bright wings," wrote Hopkins, a poet who was also a priest. The hawks were stunning, after all.

Nest Blessing

THE NEST BLESSING WAS HELD MID-WEEK, on a warm and sunny afternoon in late March. It happened that in 2010, the rituals of Holy Week and Easter sprawled across the first week of April, and the blessing could not be put off until later. By then, the hatchlings would have appeared, and the protective parents might attack Father Matt or anyone else who approached the nest.

So, March it was, and Matt performed the ritual from the lane below the nest, at a distance from Josephine, fierce protector of her clutch of eggs, and away from Armande, perched in a nearby maple, rustling his feathers on full alert for predators. A fine spring day, and some parishioners from St. Basil's Church joined the students, lining up in the lane that ran south of Brennan Hall. Elias welcomed everyone, and then Natalie stepped forward and began to sing.

She sang in praise of birds and of plants and of all living things. She sang with a beautiful soprano voice, and the sound of it drew Matt into the woods of his youth, into the memory of Valerie and her guitar, a song she had written — "Lost in My Island Time" — and the wooden bird he gave her because he'd let her be bullied and hadn't stood up for her. Valerie's singing still adrift on the breeze, a silken ribbon of sound, and in the distance, the bonging and whirring of his father's clocks that had trapped that man in the passing time. Yet he believed that

72

in memory, the past was alive and eternal, somehow redeemed and blessed inside the compassionate heart of God.

For a moment, he wondered where he was.

Natalie had stopped singing, and her silence nudged him back into the world as his eye caught something — no, someone — a slim dark-haired man in a well-tailored jacket and silk tie, one whose stylish attire stood out from the rumpled assortment of student jeans and hoodies. He wasn't taking photos, just scanning the crowd, elbows folded across his chest, a caustic look of disapproval in his eyes. Gavin Moore, he thought. The man who'd barged into his office. He wondered why he'd come.

Matt took a spruce bough and dipped it in water. "May God bless this nest," he said, "which nurtures the gift of new life."

He watched dozens of hands raise cellphones high as if they could both give a blessing and capture some radiant image of its presence as he swung his arm high, scattering droplets into the air and down on the steps before him. Looking up, he noticed that Josephine was sitting on the nest, eyeing his blessing, calm and attentive, as if she were aware of the solemnity of the occasion.

At that moment, Matt saw Armande soaring, flying eastward toward the nest, clutching a rat in his talons. He landed beside his hungry mate and began to eviscerate the rodent, tossing the unwanted bits over the edge of the roof and feeding the rest to her.

He noticed TV videocams tracking Armande. It'll be the last item on the local news, he thought. The hawk swooped above him, calling its silvery *kre-e-e-e* note. It flew low enough to cast a shadow.

Hawks are messengers, the native people say.

He'd grown fond of Armande and Josephine. He admired their detachment, their lack of complication. It touched him that he looked forward to the hatching eggs. Alison would have enjoyed the blessing, Matt thought.

Later, he mingled with guests and spoke to parishioners, struck by their interest in the nest. He noted that Gavin Moore was nowhere to be seen, and he wondered if that dapper critic had been him or someone else. Meanwhile, Elias and Natalie were giving interviews to local media. He didn't catch the stations, but at one point, he heard Elias speaking French to a reporter. He made a mental note to watch the news.

That Man

HE DECIDED TO WATCH TV LATER that evening, making his way to the lounge, knowing Father Giles would be there, tuning in to the French news. As he greeted his colleague, he saw on the screen the reporter who'd interviewed Elias. "Shall I translate?" asked the priest, and Matt said "Yes," listening to the man's rendition of Elias as he described the hawks' spectacular plumage, their dedication to the nest, the treat in store for thousands of online visitors who would observe the second brood of loveable young from Armande and Josephine.

"Oh, and here is that man," said Father Giles, laughing.

Matt wondered what he meant, until he realized that the interview had ended, and the program's anchor had returned to the screen. "He's so funny in French," said Father Giles. "Just his tone of voice. So serious, almost mocking. Listen…"

"*Le bénédiction des faucons,*" the man intoned. The blessing of the hawks.

"And look how he raises his hand to bless." Father Giles laughs as he points to the screen. "*Que Dieu vous benisse.*" Such irony in his voice. He is making fun of the whole idea."

Matt looked at the screen, startled. That face. The man's hair was white now.

"You know he reported from Rwanda," said Father Giles. "He cannot take this seriously."

75

He had not set eyes on Gerard Lefèvre in over forty years. He excused himself and left.

Gerard, his house super during that fateful summer when the man threw him out for disorderly behaviour, then married Valerie when he himself refused her. She was pregnant, but he didn't want a child. Not yet.

Gerard Lefèvre raised his son.

He was going to forget about this. Put it out of mind.

It was a condition of his acceptance into the priesthood that he never tell anyone he'd fathered a son.

He went to the campus gym, worked out, forgot it all.

Supper, then plenty of papers to mark. Then sleep.

A Note Matt Wrote to Himself

TORONTO, APRIL 1, 2010

It's Holy Week and classes are over. Exams coming up, then meetings.

The online group is watching the eggs, waiting for a pair of hatchlings, two bewildered, fluff-headed young, dark eyes full of whatever the dark eyes of a tiny bird are full of. No doubt, they'll observe them, tweet and post Facebook photos and videos on YouTube. The chat room troll has left the scene and Alison's come back (New life would probably bore that guy to tears).

It was a shock to see Gerard Lefèvre on TV, his hair white, bereaved by the loss of his son. For so long I have carried him in memory as a young man. I had forgotten this.

We are made up of so many isolated souls. School kids in classrooms, shut-in seniors, internet junkies with time on their hands.

Old folks sitting on park benches.

People who find themselves alone.

Login

LATER, AT SHOREHAVEN, Matt remembered how he would pray for the anonymous souls seated before their screens, for all those who gathered, nest-like, to encircle and protect the clutch of eggs about to hatch. He found himself praying for the eggs as well, but he would have been embarrassed to tell anyone he did.

Peregrine: Hello there, anybody home?

Kestrella: Chirp. Might as well be sitting on the nest, that's how "home" I am.

Hawkette: Two chicks hatched this morning. Aren't they beautiful?

Kestrella: Awww! Little fluffballs. Do they eat rat?

Cameraman: Fresh off the bone. Here comes dad with takeout.

Skywatcher: Hi guys. Love those chicks!

Peregrine: Little factoid: the correct name for a hawk chick is eyas.

Cameraman: *Eye-ass?* Sounds rude.

Peregrine: It's the same for falcons. I'm a Raptor Educator.

Cameraman: Wazzat?

Peregrine: I've just earned my licence to keep falcons and display them, too. Now I can take my Daisy to the schools.

Skywatcher: You've got a falcon named Daisy?

Peregrine: She was in an accident. She's very sweet-natured.

Skywatcher: We could use her in the army!

Peregrine: She'd be good company, but she can't fly well.

GSB: How long before they fledge?

Kestrella: Six weeks, maybe. Look at those teeny talons!

Skywatcher: Mama's feeding them rat bits. Look how she skewers that rat.

Natalie: Hi folks, sorry I'm late. How do you like the chicks?

Cameraman: The term is "eyas." No, it's not a cuss word.

Natalie: OK, chickadees :) It's our job to name them. How about we thank the college for letting us do this? Name the little ones Carr and Teefy.

Kestrella: Are they the Canadians who discovered penicillin?

Natalie: Uh-uh. That would be Banting and Best.

Kestrella: Oops.

Cameraman: Carr and Teefy played goalie for the Leafs!

Natalie: Carr and Teefy are two campus halls.

Cameraman: The green stuff'll roll in.

Hawkette: I feel so protective of these little ones.

Peregrine: So do I.

Hawkette: Awesome. Blessed be the birds. Shit, I still believe in God. Night, all.

What He Couldn't Write

ONE YEAR LATER, MATT BEGAN to write in his journal about the hawks' nest. He did this with hesitation, haunted by a dream he'd had of a tree nest that ended up on the town beach, one that was woven of perfection, twigs, and darkness; one that the tide — or some predator — had snatched away, its grown birds absent, its nestlings destroyed. It was as if all nests were woven of that single one, made of the same frail symmetry. All young birds emerged from its eggs, all were held in the same mysterious circle of life and death. To speak of a nest was to tread on holy ground. To write of it was to set words adrift in the tide that had drawn it away from him. All he could do was remember.

Still, he recalled good things that happened during the time of the great hawks Josephine, Armande, and their young, the growing and fledging of the two eyasses, Carr and Teefy. How the students clustered around tablets and smart phones as if they themselves were nesting parents, along with thousands online, not to mention the chat room: Cameraman teasing young Alison/Peregrine who seemed to like the attention, one or more trolls having been banished from the site; Kestrella and Hawkette *oohing* and *aahing* over the nestlings, watching as they tottered out on the Brennan Hall overhang, jumping and flapping their wings.

Skywatcher saying, "What a beautiful sight, a comfort," as

he'd just lost two buddies outside Kabul to an IED, at which point Matt thought, I know what you're going through, but he didn't write it. He didn't want to get going on Nam and maybe that was selfish. He wrung himself out over that and finally he said, "Peace, brother, I'm old enough to remember the war," and Sky said, "Thanks, GSB, you're a bud," and then he went on to say, "My heart goes out to all of you. You're good people. You don't know how much this means to me. In memory of my lost buddies, I wish the fledgling hawks good flight," and there were a lot of tears when he wrote that, even from Falco who's a tough nut, and Downtown who lost his brother on 9/11.

Everyone's got their own worst memory, thought Matt, both personal and of this world so full of mayhem. It didn't take much to set it off. He understood Sky's anguish, Downtown's grief, but he could never talk to a man who'd lost a son. Even though he himself had lost a son, it was not the same; his son was not a loved one. What right had he to live in thrall to that late-summer day of aerial homicide and collapsing towers, to cling to that prayer card that Valerie had sent him, a life raft against the surging tide of new calamities, inevitable forgetting? He should just let go of it, and yet he could not, would not.

Even so, new things had enticed him. Natalie and Elias organized a Fledge Watch for those in Toronto keeping vigil on a bench outside Brennan Hall, and it seemed as if everyone on earth must have been watching on that warm May afternoon when little Carr and then Teefy lifted their uncertain wings and flew with an amateurish, unhawkish flapping from the nest into a nearby tree where Armande was waiting with a small cache of pigeon bits to reward them. Josephine followed along, and there was a round of applause from a crowd of onlookers on the ground.

Matt had wondered what would become of the online chat, now that the eyasses were gone from the nest. It had surprised him that he cared.

Yet he did not write that down. That he cared.

Cool Wind of Silence

EASTER SUNDAY MIGHT HAVE BEEN the reason Matt stopped writing about the nest. In 2010, the feast fell on April 4, a month before the hatching of Carr and Teefy. Images drifted through memory, foretelling nothing more than a happy occasion — Sunday Mass, a mild spring day, a walk to Natalie's on St. Joseph Street for brunch.

Elias greeted him, just as one of his guests asked, "Did anyone check out Armande this morning? Flew in with a humungous dead rat and dropped it! Right on the steps of St. Basil's Church!" Laughter all around.

"And did Armande go back for it?" Matt asked.

"Either he did, or a certain college president is going to pick it up by the tail and drop it on Natalie's desk", said Elias. Howls of laughter.

Then Elias raised his hand for silence. Natalie handed him a bottle of champagne and a towel. "Easter is a time of special happiness and new life. So we have brought all of you here to let you know that we are going to be married," said Elias. "In June. Here on campus. And you are all invited." Everyone applauded while Elias popped the cork and poured champagne.

"Bravo!" said Matt, sipping his drink. Feeling mellow, he offered a toast. "To the wedding of theology and the culinary arts," he added. "With the blessing of Armande and Josephine."

Everyone raised their glasses. Matt was feeling more relaxed than usual, or it may have been the champagne. He couldn't take his eye off the photo of the young red-haired man, and when he went into the kitchen, he said to Natalie, "I hope I'm not being rude, but there's a photo of a man you resemble. Is that your uncle?"

She smiled at him. "Yes," she said. "It's an old picture, taken years ago, at his boyfriend's house."

A look crossed her face, one he knew well from parish work. *Oh my God, I'm talking to a priest. I shouldn't have said that.*

"There's a story behind it," she continued. She looked hesitant, as if she were waiting for permission to go on.

"So, tell me."

"They'd made a feast for Andre's parents," she began, "but his dad didn't make it back in time. He was a reporter, stranded in — God, I don't remember. The Middle East. Something blew up over there. Anyway, Uncle James was trying to cheer up Andre and his mom. They loved each other so much, those two men. Yes, Uncle James used to come over and bake with me. Apart from Elias, he's the kindest man I've ever known."

Matt was struck by her ease in talking. She's on her second round of champagne, he thought. *Like me.*

"Culinary mystery solved," he said. "I think you were blessed."

"I'm relieved, Matt," said Natalie. "I was shy about sharing this. Not all priests are okay around gay people."

He laughed and said, "Don't worry. I'll look forward to meeting him at your wedding."

Rather than the smile he expected, poor Natalie dropped her voice and said, "He's no longer with us. He had a career in New York, poor Uncle James..." Matt was thinking HIV/AIDS, but she said, "he was a sous-chef at the restaurant in the Twin Towers."

Matt whispered, "Oh, my God," and she went on to say that

his partner was in the opposite building. He did web design or something. Neither made it out.

Matt felt dizzy. He asked her the name of her uncle's partner, and she said, "Andre Lefèvre. His dad's an anchor on Radio-Canada. Why did you want to know?"

Matt said, "So that I can pray for them both."

The conversation ended, and Matt helped her serve the meal, but he ate little. He said he was tired and left early.

He sat on a bench in the quad and watched the hawks' nest.

He stared at the ledge above the entrance to Brennan Hall, its chiselled Gothic facade streaked with the chalky residue of bird poop.

Andre.

My son was gay.

The mother hawk was brooding on her eggs.

His mother Valerie married Gerard.

If I'd raised my son, maybe he would have been straight.

A crowd was gathering to watch the hawks. He ignored them.

He'd thought he'd gotten over this. *For God's sake you wanted her to get rid of it. She refused. You ran off to Vietnam. She found herself a husband.*

He glanced upward, and a cool wind of silence swept across him, as it does when the moon's shadow is about to eclipse the sun. He vanished into its dark penumbra. He did not wish to re-emerge in daylight.

Reverie

ONCE, HE CARVED VALERIE A TENDER BIRD, *and she became that bird and sang. She'd pull music out of the air, as if the strings of her guitar were made of light. Her music shivered inside it until he couldn't bear it anymore, until he took her inside, until he kissed her, until he undressed her, and she began to cry. But she was ready and he said, "Now," and she said, "I'm afraid," and he said, "Don't be, I love you." And he got her on the bed and together they began Andre, and she said, "I love you," and he said, "See? It's good, isn't it? Tell me it's good," and she whispered, "It's good," but he meant their pleasure, while Valerie meant what was happening inside her, what would grow between them and beyond them. And when he found out, he wanted it gone, and he almost got his way. Thank God he did not, but Andre died anyway, and now he wondered if his foul wish was a curse that pursued his innocent son and finally doomed him.*

Alone

MATT MARRIED NATALIE AND ELIAS in the student chapel under St. Basil's church, just east of Brennan Hall and the hawks' nest and the quad where the two magnificent red-tails were teaching their fledglings to hunt and fly.

"Elias, will you take Natalie to be your wife," and Matt noticed their faces alight with joy. He watched Elias take Natalie's right hand. Natalie placed her left hand on her stomach, and Matt caught the slight curve of her slender form, the life for whom these vows were made.

The couple left the chapel, then stood in the walled garden by the entrance to receive the good wishes of their families and friends. There was a reception afterwards at Brennan Hall. As the pair approached the entrance, one of the great hawks swooped down over them, calling out its elegant *kre-e-e-e* note, then ascending to the sky. "My grandfather would say that is a blessing," said Elias to the guests.

"I think it's his wedding gift," said Natalie. "A greeting from Nigeria."

"A gift of grace," said Elias.

Matt went to the reception, mixed with the guests, said a few goodbyes. He would be leaving Toronto soon, heading back to Boston, to his academic duties and to an understaffed parish in need of a part-time priest.

Elias will make a good father, he thought. *A generous man.*
You've been another sort of father, said his heart.
My last chance, that's why.
God forgives if you ask. You know that.
God forgives, but humans plant IEDs *by the roadside. One day, they explode. It's the ambush of old age, the revenge of sins that lie in wait. Life does not let you get away with anything. It's life that punishes us, not God. A loneliness we bring upon ourselves.*
God may forgive, but life sets things in motion. Evil things. I missed the plane that killed my son. Life granted me the seed of a wish I planted long ago.
He had found a calling, good work for his soul. Even so.
It was too shameful a tale to tell, how he abandoned his lover and his son. "God found you, isn't that enough?" asked his superior.
Typical priest-talk.
No, it wasn't.
God may have found you first, but it was life that found you in the end, tackled you and pinned you down with a knockout punch. He could hear the count of the referee, the clang of the final bell, the crowds cheering, but not for him.
He'd be alone for the rest of his life.

Prayerful Bird

IN JUNE 2010 — LESS THAN A YEAR before he fell ill — Matt returned to Boston, to weekday Mass at St. Bartholomew's Church. Vested and in the sacristy, he viewed ten or so parishioners, hesitant as they made their way to their seats, life slowing most of them down with canes and walkers. He needed to find someone able to carry the bread and wine to the altar. *Alison. She'll be here for sure.*

He waited, and in a few moments, Alison arrived.

He stared at her.

Daisy, the falcon, was riding on her gloved fist. Alison walked to a pew at the rear, genuflected with a dancer's grace, then took her seat. She was as serene as a lake at dawn. Yet Matt could not have known that this practice began when Alison first took Daisy to Mass to pray in thanksgiving for her Raptor Educator's Licence. So well-behaved was the little falcon that her keeper decided to continue the practise. She had felt certain that in a half-empty church, there would not be enough people to object to Daisy or to make her fuss. Tethered, she would perch on Alison's glove, remaining unruffled throughout the Mass, confining her activity to the occasional deposit on the garbage bag that Alison had spread on the pew beside her.

As she pondered this, Alison saw Father Matt coming out of the sacristy, down the aisle, approaching her. He looked fretful.

"And this is...?"

"Daisy. My little one."

"We've never had a falcon in church."

Alison could tell that he felt ridiculous, saying this. "I believe that Daisy is a prayerful creature," she said.

"And you take her to Mass?"

"She is never more quiet, more attentive. And no one seems to mind."

And no one sits next to you, either, Matt thought.

Matt found someone else to bring the gifts to the altar. Daisy was well-behaved and did not fuss.

I'm just filling in at St. Bart's, Matt thought. *It's not my responsibility.*

The Mass proceeded and at Communion time, Alison approached the altar with Daisy on her arm, enfolded in a calm, mysterious elation, a luminous beauty that Matt almost never saw in the frazzled distractedness of typical communicants. She seemed to claim a sense of rightness about the world. She opened her free hand to receive the bread from Father Matt.

"Will you bless Daisy?" she asked him.

It is highly irregular, he thought. Blessings were reserved for children or for adults preparing to receive the sacrament. There was nothing in canon law that allowed a bird to be blessed during Communion.

Yet his hand wanted to bless. He held it over the bird's head. "Bless you," he whispered.

He hoped no one would complain.

After Mass, he returned to the sacristy, a bit unnerved but also amused by the fact that a handicapped falcon had found a way around his rational faculties. He'd never intended to bless that bird. He wondered about Alison, her unearthly air, the way she'd opened a space for herself and her feathered companion, as if she were Moses, parting seas to find a path to safety. Only what did that make him? Not quite part of Pharaoh's army, in pursuit of renegades and drowned in the flood. Nothing that dire. Just a perplexed observer; that was all.

He saw Alison standing at the back of the church, as if she knew he wanted to speak to her. "Father Matt, I'm sorry if I embarrassed you," she said. "I should have asked beforehand."

"We aren't supposed to bless birds at Communion."

He thought his own statement so ridiculous that he was afraid he might laugh.

"I understand," said Alison. "I won't ask again. Besides, it's only a sign. God has already blessed Daisy."

"Even if I had refused," he said.

"God blessed her with another chance at life."

I shouldn't even allow that bird in church, he thought. This thought leapt, involuntarily, to his mind, as if he were reading from a script. In truth, he did not see a problem with Daisy, beyond the one that Alison managed with a garbage bag.

"And she is grateful," Alison continued. "She responds as a prayerful bird."

Matt didn't answer. He wasn't sure how to react to a comment like that. Instead, he informed her that there would be a proper animal blessing in October, on the feast of St. Francis.

Oddballs

ALISON CONTINUED ATTENDING DAILY MASS whenever she could, and she began to bring Daisy (and her garbage bag) to the ten a.m. Sunday liturgy. While no one was unfriendly, she would always end up with most of the pew to herself. Gentle Daisy had a fearsome profile and the falcon's cruel reputation. Parishioners, there for an hour of tranquillity, could not help but notice her curved beak, her sharp talons, her fierce raptor's eyes.

Aware of this, Alison wrote an article for the online parish bulletin, called, "A Word About Daisy." She told the story of the falcon's near-death and miraculous recovery, including a link to the South Boston Animal Shelter website. After that, a few young, eco-friendly parishioners stopped to talk to her and Daisy after Mass, albeit with a certain amount of caution. The more devout, older folk believed that Daisy was a sign of God's love made manifest in creation. Almost everyone thought Alison strange, but there were plenty of oddballs in the parish, street people who talked to themselves and shouted incoherent statements during the Mass. Yet the pastor wanted his parishioners to be inclusive, diverse and what-all, so they put up with the falcon and her keeper, and left it at that.

Hashtag

MATT KNEW A LOT ABOUT DAISY from the chat room in Toronto, and he'd concluded that Alison was a bit strange. Home again in Boston, faced with his own distress and the barrenness of his life, he thought again. He regretted the way he had dismissed the kind of free-range spirituality that clucked over every New-Age seed and crumb in the barnyard, untutored as it was in the nourishment of formal theology. He was too exhausted for those old cerebral gymnastics. Alison was strange but happy. She had a genuine apprehension of grace, he knew that.

He'd thought at first that Alison might have a calling to religious life, one to which he might direct her, once she got tired of Daisy.

Then, she sent him a link to her Twitter feed.

@AlisonPeregrine
#PrayingWithYourFalcon.
31,285 followers.

She was tweeting short, bird-based prayers all over cyberspace.

@AlisonPeregrine Bless the falcon, whose eyes see more than ours. A creature made in the image of God.
#PrayingWithYourFalcon.

Well, okay. She was touching people's souls, getting into musty crevices of the psyche that he could never reach. His old world was over. Books, lectures, interviews, even pastoral psychology couldn't quite do that. He had to believe that the sacraments still could.

Social media was for sociable people. It wasn't quite his thing.

He realized that he missed Elias and Natalie. *Their new life, I'm sure, is going well. They'll have a child by the end of the year. I should email them. Find out how the fledglings are doing. Carr and Teefy.*

At this distance, the whole bird-nest caper felt dreamlike, as if it had never happened. Daisy's appearance at Mass seemed like a weird spinoff, a bit of viral dandruff that Alison picked up in the chat room. Yet he couldn't bring himself to forbid the falcon's presence in church. Daisy's life had been saved, just as his had been.

Your life is worth more than many sparrows.

Scraps and Bones

HE, TOO, HAD ALMOST LOST HIS LIFE, and so he felt some compassion for the poor, injured bird that Alison loved.

After he had missed his plane on that dreadful September morning, a retreat director told him that he must take heart, that his life was embraced by God; that just as Matt loved the birds of the air, so did God love him. None of this explained why so many innocent lives had been lost; why his, with all its scars and wounds, should have been saved more than once. Even so, he could sense the mystery of a benign presence in a wretched world, of loving kindness sifting down through the cracks in broken lives like sunlight through a dense layering of trees, touching the dark wooded places of the psyche. He could not ridicule Alison and her falcon when gracious life had taken him in hand, had saved him, more than once.

He decided to walk in Boston's Public Garden, becoming lost in the dazzle of midday June, its lush and florid vegetation, light shimmering on the tips of sword-like fronds, bayonets, a jungle war, the one he joined to avenge his father. The man was a World War Two vet, a dazed ex-POW who'd sold bric-a-brac at a junkshop called Victory Hardware, who tinkered with bizarre clocks and unproven systems of time. A man who stared at his son, when shown his draft notice, heartbreak and terror etched on his aging face like a worn map of the path life had taken him to nowhere.

"Rip it up," said his dad.

"Right. And get thrown in jail."

"Jail's better than going to war. Go to Canada."

"Canada's for chickenshits. You guys were brave. But you didn't get to finish the job."

"That 'job' will never be finished," said his dad.

He thought his dad was tired, unable to defend his reasoning. "I want to do what you couldn't do," he told him.

"Matt..." his father hesitated. "There are better ways to serve your country."

Only Matt had lived his life with a father in profound despair, a man who'd been held prisoner and who no longer knew how to fight back. So grieved was he by the man's suffering, so lonely in the presence of his emptiness that his sorrow calcified into a silent fury at the world and its injustice. He wanted to redeem his father's anguish, the hot iron brand that had scarred his soul.

He went to Vietnam. One month into his tour of duty, he got word of his father's death.

Truth was, he was terrified of fatherhood. He didn't know how to be a father. He had to flee Valerie and his unborn child so he went to war, lit up his veins with drugs until he saw the shattered galaxies of night, the enemy's face enormous and pale as the moon, until he found himself screaming, "Kill him, kill him." A buddy. An innocent soldier. After this, his war was over. He was sent home to a mother who wondered whose son this was.

Alone and distraught, he snorted speed, floating away from the torment of memory until the drug gripped him, chained his body to the habit. No longer floating free, he took too much, found himself nervous, jumpy, terrified, until one evening he sped along the Tappan Zee Bridge that spanned the Hudson River. Then, just as quickly, he pulled over, the waters below inviting him in. One leg went over the bridge, then another, his outstretched arms gripping the spandrels, and he heard a voice saying, "You don't have to die, buddy, it's already been taken care of," and then he felt the grip of arms and hands, of cops grabbing him, pulling him away from his lost soul.

He ended up in a psychiatric ward, his parish priest the only friend he had until he got well, until he was free of his addiction. Then, he was restless. Restored to life after killing an innocent man, he wanted to give something back to the world he'd injured. He began to think about the priesthood.

Yet he could still feel Valerie's presence, smell the fragrance of her lavender perfume. Valerie was married now. He told the priest about her. He prayed to be relieved of longing.

"What were the words you heard that night on the bridge?" asked the vocations director when he went to see him.

"You don't have to die, buddy, it's already been taken care of."

"God was trying to tell you something," the man said. "That you have been saved by his Son."

"I was on drugs," said Matt.

"God works with whatever scraps and bones he can. He saved your life."

You Don't Get Out Enough

THE FALCON WOULD TEACH HIM HUMILITY, he thought. Daisy's life had also been saved — and, in fact, the life of her entire species, once endangered, their eggshells thinned by DDT. It had not been God's plan, he thought, that either Daisy or her kind should perish, and no doubt Alison was meant to do her small share of providential work.

And what about him? Perhaps less worthy than Daisy — whose catastrophic fall was accidental — was a man who had tried to leap to his death. Yet worthiness did not seem to matter. Man and bird had been restored to life; man and bird had been given the same extraordinary gift.

As a priest, he'd come to understand that he had no privileged insight, no special claim on wisdom. Yet it troubled him to realize that he could not grasp the meaning of his own existence, the fate he shared with the likes of Daisy.

Although he loved birds, Matt found that the periods of spring and fall migrations were crowded with marking papers and committee work, and so he seldom found time for excursions, for viewing the arrivals and departures of warblers, the spiralling of hawks and eagles. Now at Mass, he was faced with a wild creature in the care of a young woman, her serene yet haunted face confronting him with the absence of calm in his life, with a fear of the wilderness inside him.

At Mass, he could feel both the falcon and her keeper, their luminous eyes tracking him across the altar, scanning him in wonder. In their presence, he began to feel insubstantial, like a phantom of the computer — an image formed of colour and light, pixels easily deleted.

Because it was summer, he had some down time. Alone in his office, he read.

A Rage for Falcons got jammed with sticky notes, and *Falconry Basics: A Handbook for Beginners* (already battered by a previous owner) ended up with loose pages and a cracked spine. This was followed by *Understanding the Bird of Prey*, which he filled with marginalia. For relief from his academic habits, he went online and watched raptor videos from Cornell, then discovered a Facebook Hawkaholics page, which, among other things, posted memorials in incorrect Latin to fledgling "hawklets" killed on their maiden voyages.

He went back to his reading. Only he was too restless to concentrate.

You don't get out enough, he thought.

He wanted to be blessed by strange golden eyes, by the feel of a cape of feathers and a beating heart. He was afraid to let anyone know this.

Turning again to his computer, he googled, "raptor displays, Massachusetts."

The Number of Things Beyond Him

MATT DONNED CIVVIES AND TOOK an afternoon off, travelling by bus to central Massachusetts. He was headed for the Green Valley Falconry Centre, where he hoped to get acquainted with a creature much like Daisy.

He'd set up the meeting in advance with a guide, a trained falconer named Pete who briefed him on what to expect, then introduced him to Clipper, a male lanner falcon, a breed much like the peregrine, but somewhat larger in size. Pete showed him how to handle the tethers and how to balance the falcon on his glove. Walking him past the bird enclosures, Pete brought Matt into the supply room where he opened the fridge and removed a small plastic bag containing dead white mice.

"I'll let you carry these," he said. "Give you the real feel."

Of what? Matt wondered.

"Clipper enjoys these treats," Pete said.

The chilled mice appeared compact, uniform in size, small and rectangular. Matt thought of white chocolate. Dubious, he hesitated only for a moment before tucking the zip-lock bag into his pocket. *I bet Alison carries these everywhere.* He cringed at the thought that she might be feeding chewy little white mice to Daisy at the back of the church.

Why do you think Daisy's so calm?

With some trepidation, Matt bore the falcon on his arm and walked with Pete along a wooded path. The creature was light, almost featherweight. "Hollow-boned," the guide explained, "for ease of flying." Matt gazed at its small face as he had never gazed at Daisy, and he saw the intensity of its blue-black eyes and their golden rings, noting a dazed perfection in the creature's bearing, its slate-grey feathers, creamy throat, striated breast. It was as if, still in its youth, the young raptor did not grasp the enormity of its being. In awe, he watched it, knowing he could never comprehend this creature nor could any human on this earth. It belonged to God alone, to God's purpose and intent for it.

At that moment, as if to concur, Clipper raised his elegant wings, stretched his golden talons, fanned his tail, and Matt made the slight movement of his forearm needed to help balance the creature and settle it down.

"Well done," said Pete.

Yet at that moment, he felt inadequate, out of his depth.

"Lanner falcons take well to the glove," the man continued. "Maybe you'd like to feed him."

That beak, Matt thought. *He could bite my finger off.*

He should have thought of that sooner. He would have a terrible time celebrating the Eucharist if he suffered a falcon amputation.

He dug into his pocket, pulled out one of the mice by the tail and held it out to Clipper. The falcon snapped it up and swallowed it whole.

"Good boy," Matt said.

But this is not a dog, Matt thought. *Maybe this is just plain beyond me.*

Yet it was not beyond Alison. Nor was it beyond Pete the falconer, licenced to keep these raptors in good health, to attend to their needs. Both Pete and Alison brought these simple creatures happiness, in whatever way God gave falcons to understand that state of mind.

He was surprised at the number of things that were beyond him.

Matt asked Pete if he knew Alison, and yes, he'd met her. He thought she was an excellent raptor educator, and when Pete asked how he knew her, Matt was somewhat embarrassed to admit the truth: that he was a priest in her parish, that Alison brought Daisy to Mass with her, and he needed to be better informed about the falcon and her needs.

"We live in that kind of a world now," said Pete. "Animals are people, too." And he laughed.

On the bus back to Boston, Matt felt unsettled. He should pray in thanksgiving, he thought — even if Clipper's spirit was beyond his grasp. He should thank God anyway.

Matt pulled out his smart phone. As if I knew God's email address, he thought. He had email from Twitter, the popular posts in his network. Alison's was first.

> @AlisonPeregrine My father wrote: All of it mystery, all of it a gift.
> Shelter me, God of tender wings. I nest in You.
> #PrayingWithYourFalcon.

When Matt put the phone back in his pocket, he felt the bag of mice treats, still there.

Old Soul

ON HIS WAY TO ST. BART'S for Sunday Mass, Matt saw Alison crossing the Common. He had expected to see her, and so he remembered to bring the packet of mice, chilled and ready for Daisy. How spectral the young woman looked — an ancient apparition of nobility, her hair woven into a crown of braids, a falcon resting on her fist. Queens, he recalled, were allowed to train specific birds for falconry, although he could not remember which ones. Not that it mattered. What troubled him was Alison's ghostly appearance, as if she had somehow loosened the bonds of time, as if by looking at her, he was gazing into the past. Or perhaps this was the falcon's doing, some special dispensation he could not fathom.

Alison seemed absorbed in thought as he approached her. He said hello.

"I wanted to tell you," he began, "that I spent a day at the Green Valley Falconry Centre."

"You met Pete?"

"Yes, and he's very knowledgeable. Excellent," said Matt. "And Clipper is a remarkable bird."

Alison paused. "Clipper has a very old soul," she said at last. "I think he was present at the Creation."

"You mean in the Garden of Eden?"

Alison looked confused for a moment by Matt's joke.

"I don't know," she said at last, her voice sad.

By way of reassurance, Matt told her that Clipper was a special bird. He offered her the bag of mice for Daisy. Then he told her that he'd just received an email from Cameron Reilly, a.k.a. Cameraman, who'd be giving a talk at Harvard.

"From our chat room?" Her eyes widened. "Daisy and I are reading his book."

"He'll enjoy meeting both of you," said Matt.

They would never let Daisy in the door, she thought.

"I'd like to invite him to speak at the church," said Matt.

Alison looked relieved. "Daisy," she whispered. "Cam wants to meet you."

At that moment, Matt felt as if she had drawn a translucent veil around herself and her falcon, vanishing into a place of safety, far from him. She whispered something to Daisy, but Matt did not hear it. He felt as if she were about to disappear.

Matt watched Alison as she slipped through the trees like a needle threading an imagined world through the fabric of the real. Drifting over to a park bench, she sat down beside an unshaven, derelict man, a bundle buggy beside him and a cup for the spare change of passersby. God knows what he's spending it on, Matt thought. *Booze and drugs*. And then he felt ashamed of his tendency to harsh judgment, because Alison reached down and put money in that cup. Alison needs protection from her innocence, he thought. She had begun a conversation with the man, showing off Daisy who lifted her wings, and he thought that one or both of them might be angelic, beloved of God, unsuited to live in this terrible world.

Alison

From Alison's Journal

I TOOK ON DAISY IN MEMORY of my father, who loved raptors, while I was a child and afraid of them. Many years later, Providence sent me a wounded falcon to heal and to love. She is wild. She belongs to no human, only to God.

I sense that in her own way, Daisy is a meditative creature. I believe she is capable of love.

Yes, I know that sounds ridiculous. It is not always easy to match my sense of things to language. I am trying to convey some of the joy that Daisy brings me. She encourages detachment. She lives inside the mystery of her own life.

I guess I upset Fr. Matt, bringing her to church, then asking him to bless her. Yet I don't intend to leave her at home. She is holy, the breath and wind of God. She belongs in church, if only to confront its stone doors, bolted shut against the living world.

Soon

ALISON SAID GOODBYE TO THE MAN in the park and continued walking. "That poor fellow's having a hard time, Daisy. He needs a friend." Daisy was fussing in the hot weather, straining against the jesses, the soft, ribbon-like tethers less of a problem than the humidity. Alison stroked her chest with the back of her hand. "Soon, you'll meet Cameron," she said to the restless creature. "You must be kind to him. He is also in need of consolation, I could sense this in the chat room." Daisy settled down as if to absorb this, but Alison was startled by her own thoughts, even afraid of them — unaware until that very moment that while online, she'd allowed herself to feel for the soul of a man she'd never met.

Daisy

CAGED, DAISY RESTED IN THE EASY COMFORT of the night, eyes on her keeper, light feathering her body. The woman held up something large. Daisy eyed it.

"I'm reading a book by Cameron Byrne," she said. "*At Work in the Fields of the New Cosmology.*"

Puzzled, Daisy turned her head in the direction of the voice.

Her keeper smiled. "You know I'm talking to you. You are so smart."

Daisy felt kindness, the warmth of it like sunlight. From her perch, she stood tall and flapped her wings.

"Happy?"

A gloved hand, then the cage door opening.

"Up, up, Daisy."

Daisy leapt to her glove, felt the gentle touch of a hand against her head.

"Happy Daisy. There's a good girl."

Her keeper lifted a small black object. "Look this way, sweetheart." Daisy did, saw the light flash.

Alison sat with her in the warm lamplight. Daisy could not think *happy*, only feel the gentle weight of human language as it shaped the air around her, its tender softness lighting on her body. She raised her eyes to her keeper and met her kindly gaze until the woman kissed her tufted head, then placed her back in her cage. "Sleep well, Daisy."

She lowered the curtain. Darkness fell.

@AlisonPeregrine Daisy watches me read on the New Cosmology. A silent, meditative creature. Beautiful book by Cameron Byrne. #PrayingWithYourFalcon

@AlisonPeregrine Daisy lifts her wings in praise. Compassionate God, brooding on the world, hide us in the shelter of your wing. #PrayingWithYourFalcon

Sleepless

IN NEW YORK, CAMERON BYRNE felt drenched by the humid night. He got up, checked his email, then Facebook and Twitter. His eyes widened. Alison, from the chat room. "Peregrine." He texted her.

Alison's phone pinged. *At this hour?*

> 2 nite owls. Glad U R enjoying the book. Luv yer prayers. May God bless Daisy. Be in Boston soon. Cam

"Daisy," she whispered. "Someone has sent you a blessing."

The following morning, Alison received the email announcement of Cam's upcoming lecture at Harvard. She recalled a man from the chat room who from time to time let slip some poignant detail about his past. A body humming with sorrow; she could feel it then. She stared at his photo on the email poster. Sun glinting on caramel hair, blue eyes behind rimless glasses. Something wrong, something unsteady in his look, like the flicker and dimming of electric lights before the system crashes.

Cameraman

HE HUNG OUT IN CENTRAL PARK, Washington and Tompkins Squares, one of those who photograph New York's red-tailed hawks and spreads the word online. Downtown from Fordham University he came, lugging his videocam, having told his class, "Don't just panic about fracking, climate change, nuclear leaks, decimation of the polar bear. Start by falling in love with the world. Keep dropping your jaw until it aches with wonder. You need hope, for Chrissakes."

Only, he's a theologian, so he doesn't cuss. He teaches ecotheology, the green shoot from the tree of the Cross. The sacred cosmos: sacrificial, bloodied and resurrected. He doesn't understand any of it, just knows it to be true. "The Mystery of Faith," they used to call it. But life is beyond him in its beauty and its cruelty. He's seen too much of it. He loathes the word "healing," calls it dime-store nonsense from the card rack at Walgreens. At this stage in life, the heart's a damn fist of scars. God knows what keeps the little sucker slamming in his chest.

He misses the loopy chat room up in Toronto. Great Speckled Bird, a.k.a. Father Matt; Skywatcher signing in from Afghanistan, and Alison (Peregrine) who talked about Daisy, her educational bird with asymmetrical wings. Just about all of his students followed Alison@AlisonPeregrine on Twitter. Nutty, bite-sized nibbles of faith is how he thinks of those tweets: *Daisy is a prayerful bird. God broods upon the world.*

He shows his class a DVD about the New Cosmology: all the great eco-theologians telling earth's story from the huge eruption in light that has never ended; the computer simulations of the world made new; the terrible wonder of star formation; asteroids smashing into molten Planet Earth. Colliding galaxies exploding into the devastation of "bombs bursting in air" somewhere near Fallujah, a roadside IED that tore apart an armoured vehicle, grated skin, bone shards, flesh of his flesh, his only son Tom. Six years ago, it happened. After this, his beloved wife Elaine, who'd been diagnosed with leukemia, realized she could not endure, and didn't.

Even after all this time, he sees a shrink.

Never mind. His photo blog had two thousand followers. People knew him, came up and said hello. He was never alone for long.

Cam goes to one of his three favourite parks, sets up his camera, checks his settings, trains his telephoto lens on the classical pediment of an old apartment building, a perch for the elegant spread of a red tail, one adult hawk in a state of contemplation, the other on the wing, returning with a squirrel in its talons, food to cache for their fledgling young. Gorgeous shots, fearful beauty, born to devour "this flesh for the life of my young," and he realizes that he's not up to nature's power, not today. He's spent, like the bones of Ezekiel's vision, dry and shaken by wind. *Shall these bones live?* Exhausted, he sits on the park bench, head in his hands.

He dozes off, dreams of a woman bearing a falcon.

Sitting up again, he opens his eyes, feels consoled as he packs up his camera and goes home.

It Just Happened This Way, Really

PONDERING ALISON'S TWEETS from the night before, Cam went to his office and opened an email from guess who, Great Speckled Bird, a.k.a. Father Matt Reilly in Boston, asking if he might have time to give a talk while in town, with a focus on photo-blogging and ecotheology.

"Your theological insight is much admired in our parish and elsewhere," said the priest. "In particular, one of our parishioners may be familiar to you from our chat room last spring. Alison is a licensed Raptor Educator and will probably bring her tame and tethered falcon to the event."

Cameron blinked, read it again.

He banged out an answer. "Yesyesyesyesyesyesyes." He deleted it, took a deep breath and began again: "I would be delighted to accept your invitation."

The Sky Inside

MATT WORRIED ABOUT ALISON. He felt that there was something not quite right with her, alone with only a bird for company. Now and again, he remembered the unwanted attention she'd received in the chat room from a troll who claimed to know her. It hadn't crossed his mind before now that there might have been some unpleasant sexual incident in Alison's past, one that had frightened her away from the chat room for a time, making her shy and reclusive around men. Yet whatever the case, she held down a responsible job, loved the sick and injured animals that came to the shelter, gave much of her spare time to the parish. She was innocent and kindly, yet perplexing and, he felt, quite sad. She needs friends, he thought. When Cameron arrived at the church, Matt promised to introduce him to Alison. He sensed that Cam had become like a brother to her, and judging from his memory of the chat room, she seemed at ease with him. "An unusual person," he said to Cam. "I'd like to know your impressions."

On the evening of Cam's lecture, Matt greeted Alison as she walked into the church with Daisy on her gloved fist. Indifferent to startled looks, she said hello, eyed an empty pew in back, and spread a garbage bag to her left, positioning it under Daisy.

"Talk about planning ahead," said a man's voice.

She looked up, surprised. His eyes were crinkled up with laughter and when he opened them wide, they were blue and full of sky. Their depths startled her. "Cameron Byrne," he said, and he shook her free hand. She introduced herself.

"So, this is Daisy,"

"Yes. She's my little one."

"I hope she'll enjoy the talk."

"She will. She's very intelligent. She won't fuss."

He said he hoped to talk to her afterwards.

Alison did not want to converse with him. The reality of his presence reminded her that she was not one for company. She had nothing to offer but emptiness: a locked room, a place she would neither visit nor describe.

But you talk to Father Matt, she told herself.

Not about anything much.

The space within had been filled by God with the silence of the falcon, its haunted, far-seeing eyes.

I've got nothing but the sky inside of me.

An open window.

See for yourself.

Her Father

CAMERON'S PHOTOS: MAGNIFICENT red-tailed hawks in flight, sunlight gleaming on their wings; the colourful brilliance of warblers; endangered piping plovers scraping out nests in the damp sand.

Alison watched, listened, feeling as if she were seeing on the screen the wonderful pictures that her mother had taken and brought home to her father, and then she heard the rhythmic incantation of her father's voice. "Before we were born, the great hawks came. Before we could speak, there was the silent language of the goshawk's flight, the terrible power of the falcon's speed, the elegant fanning of the red-tailed hawk. All of it a mystery, all of it a gift. Blessed be God, who broods upon the world. We nest in God."

Only she did not know whose voice she was hearing, could not recall if her father had said this or if she'd come upon it in his writings. The man who stood before her was not like her reserved and gentle father. It was as if Cameron were plugged into a hidden power source, a high-voltage current that lit up his words and maybe even frizzed his golden honeycomb of hair. He wore rimless glasses that kept tilting sideways and slipping down his nose, as if, absorbed in some exciting speculation, he might have gone and crashed into a building.

Like my poor Daisy, Alison thought. *Her first flight was her last.*

Long ago, my father was a falconer. I miss him still. He used to say that falcons know when one is in need of solace. Even with her injury, Daisy has a gift for us.

Daisy turned her gaze to Alison.

She understands me.

From the back of the room, she could feel Cam's eyes on her. *I don't want him to see me.* She did not think these words. That feeling was in her skin.

When the lecture and question period were over, she got up, took Daisy in hand, and slipped out the door.

"I don't know where she went," said Matt.

"Odd," said Cam. "I told her I wanted to talk with her."

"It could be the heat," said Matt. "She had a fainting spell not long ago."

It wasn't true. Matt felt an urge to protect her, so he made that up. He had no idea why she'd run.

To: cameraman@fordhamu.edu
From: FrMatt@bu.edu
Re: Alison
Date: July 14, 2010

Cam, you might catch Alison tomorrow. She's at the Boston Nature Center all this week in the afternoon. Click on bostonnaturecenter. com/directions.
Matt

On the other hand, Matt thought later, if he had meant to protect her privacy, why was he passing this information on to Cam?

Because something about her nags at me, he thought. *Trained in psychology and I can't make sense of her.*

Either that, or I'm afraid to.
That thought had not occurred to him before.

Solace

ALISON SAT WITH DAISY, at the centre of an outdoor gathering under the trees, leaves edged with sunlight, teenage counsellors, and squirming day-campers gathered around her, and she felt quite young, as young as her charges, as if she were seated in a child's chair at school, surrounded by big blocks and plush toys, a poor fit for the world of adulthood. It wasn't the first time she'd felt she'd gotten lost on the way to growing up, a waif with an injured falcon for a friend.

Yet she loved working with children, so she composed herself, sitting in the middle of the group with Daisy on her gloved fist, explaining to the kids what a falcon was, how it flew and hunted, how fast it could fly. "What do you feed Daisy?" "Does she bite?" "Can she sing?" "How old is she?" While she answered questions, the kids raised their phones, beckoning to Daisy, and she obliged by turning her head in their direction.

It was at one of these moments that Alison noticed Cam. He was standing at the edge of the crowd, leaning against the thick bark of a huge oak tree, only half-visible. Camouflaged. Shy, like a long-eared owl, she thought. *I don't like people who hide themselves. What is he doing here?*

She wondered how she could avoid him. Yet he did not seem in a hurry to disturb her.

As the session ended, Cam moved through the thinning crowd, and when he reached her, he told her he was driving through the area, that Father Matt had mentioned the good work she was doing with raptor education, that he'd been curious about Daisy since their time in the chat room, that he just wanted to say hello.

"Hello," she said.

"Could we walk a bit with Daisy?"

Alison hesitated. "Okay."

"I enjoyed the chat room," said Cam. "It was a great distraction."

"From what?"

"Well, life in general."

She could tell he was startled by the directness of her look, by the way she could shake a handful of stuck words loose.

He told her more about his son who'd died in Iraq, about the loss of his wife.

"What a terrible shock."

"Yeah, well. Life throws curveballs."

She stopped walking. "Would you like to hold Daisy?"

"You sure?"

"She offers great solace."

She pulled an extra glove from her pocket, and with great care, she handed him the tethers, showing him how to hold them as she rested the bird on his wrist. Daisy reared upwards, fanning the air with her outstretched wings. Cam shifted his arm, and Daisy adjusted her footing, folded her wings and settled down. "Now don't fuss," Alison whispered.

She could sense that Cam was moved by the falcon — golden-eyed, slate-winged, a creature redolent of wind and fire.

"I see why you love her," he said at last.

"It's because of my father. He was a falconer once," she said.

They meandered along in silence. Then Cam told her that Daisy's lightness held a kind of tranquility new to him. He saw that the bird did not acknowledge him in any way; she gave him only the gift of her presence, her fullness of life. She was, perhaps, everything that God might have intended of a falcon. Claws and talons and majestic wings — and for all her predatory power, innocent.

"Yes, she is a gentle bird." Alison didn't know what else to say. Cam returned Daisy to her. "I feel better already," he said.

"I apologize." She looked at him. "You're very eloquent. I don't know how to respond to you."

"It's okay."

She felt as if she were about to cry, as if she'd been stung by her own words, by the pain of some grievous longing that wracked her body as she uttered them. *I don't know how to respond.* Yet she wanted to have friends. She was afraid to have friends. "I feel you understand Daisy," she said at last.

He told her yes, that he admired her devotion to her falcon. She could relate to someone who cared for Daisy. She felt most people were afraid of her falcon, or thought she was weird for keeping one. Alison thanked him for his kindness, sure he saw his own grief reflected in her eyes.

He stopped walking and turned to face her. "Alison," he said, "I have something I want to give you."

She felt afraid.

"I would like to be your friend. And Daisy's."

Daisy was watching Cam while he took Alison's free hand and pressed it between his. For a moment, Cam had the distressing sensation that Alison had become feral, a wild creature, terrified and skittish—that unable to swim, she was drowning in the fast currents of her own estrangement, that his hand was trying to pull her back to shore.

"That's all I'll ever ask of you," he said. "Just friendship."

Daisy looked at Alison, inclining her head in Cam's direction. Alison glanced at the falcon, then at Cam. "We all need friends," she said.

All Are Welcome, Sort Of

MATT HAD ASKED CAM FOR HIS IMPRESSIONS of Alison, so he wasn't surprised when the man showed up at his Boston College office. He had come to drop off copies of his books, but he hadn't much else to offer. "I'd say she's very shy, that's all," he said.

"I don't know what to make of her."

"How so?"

"St. Bart's is an openminded parish. No one asks too many questions. 'All are welcome,' as the song goes: homeless people, panhandlers, LGBTQ, and Daisy, the Falcon." He paused. "I don't meddle where I'm not asked. She never mentions family. I suspect something there."

"She needs someone ... to ... be a friend to her, Matt. That's all."

"She's well-liked in the parish." The priest eyed him. "But what are you getting at?"

"Nothing. Just ... "

"Just watch it. She's twenty years your junior." Matt was taken aback by his own words. "I would be careful is all I'm saying."

"Alison's just a kid. I know that."

"Okay, so it's not about Alison. It's Daisy you're nuts about."

"Matt, she *prays* with Daisy."

"And you follow her on Twitter, right?" Matt saw that Cam

felt stung. "I hope you know I'm kidding," he said, unsure if he was. He wished his colleague a good trip back to New York as Cam excused himself and stomped out of the building.

There was a bus stop in front of the church. A few waiting people turned bewildered looks on the wild-haired man striding by, glasses askew, hands knotted into fists.

Reading

To: cameraman@fordham.edu
From: alison@sbas.com
Re: Your book
Date: July 17, 2010

Hi Cam,
Just a quick email to thank you for your kind words of friendship.
Could you tell me where I might find your earlier book, *The Birds of the Air*? Amazon doesn't have everything, after all, and neither do our local booksellers.
Daisy is happy and making the rounds of summer schools and camps. I'm sure that your visit was a high point in her young life.
I hope your classes go well in the fall. I keep you in my prayers.
Alison

A few days later, Alison received a parcel with a copy of the book. Cam had attached a note. "It's hard to locate old books these days," he'd written. "Please accept this as a gift." He'd signed the book, "To my friend and fellow birder, Alison. With best wishes, Cameron Byrne."

Before she began to read it, she said her father's prayer: "*Blessed be God, who broods upon the world. May we nest in God.*"

At home, she placed the book on a table beside a bowl of

flowers, a sprig of Easter palm, two of Daisy's feathers, and a crucifix. Later that evening, she sat down and began to read it. She read all night.

Matthew

What Alison Does

SHE'S STRUCK UP A FRIENDSHIP *with Cam Byrne*. Matt felt an unexpected pang, a feeling close to jealousy, that the man would have a relationship, however innocent, with Alison. He imagined the sort of dialogue he should have begun himself as a spiritual advisor. More to the point, he recalled the chat room, where he'd sensed an ease between Alison and Cam, a casual way of speaking that he could never master with anyone.

Cam was comfortable with who he was, while Matt observed the world from the prison of his body. He did not like to be reminded of this.

He tried watching Alison through the eyes of Father Ron, the pastor.

"She sits with the homeless people in the Common," Ron told him. "She tells them Daisy stories and a lot of our parishioners used to freak out over street people and now they don't. They follow her and Daisy out the door."

He did not experience the same ease. In a hurry, he often strode past vagrant men and women on park benches in the Common, and he hated to admit that to his ear, the sound of a shaking hand rattling change in a paper cup felt close to reptilian, a rattler's noise, a warning of a poisonous bite if he got too close. Worse were the mutterings: "There goes Father Cheapskate." He never dwelled on his instinctive reaction or the anger stirred in him by a sarcastic remark. Instead, he hurried down the path, off to whatever appointment (real or hoped-for) that might await him in the rectory.

Yet he felt he had to respond to Father Ron's observations. So, it happened that one Sunday after the ten a.m. Mass, he watched as parishioners filed out of St. Bart's. Alison was among them, Daisy perched on her gloved fist. She was walking alone in the direction of the Boston Common, and behind her, a mass of chattering individuals managed to shape itself into a slender line of walkers, trimming away the indolence of an hour in the pew — ready, it seemed, for some grown-up form of communion. Yes, he knew it was a cruel judgment, especially from a priest, but parish liturgies were often repetitious, and so, it never surprised him when many congregants responded with looks of utter stupefaction. All the more reason for the astonishment he felt that this crowd would be energized enough to fall into line behind Alison and Daisy.

He decided to follow them. Clad in civvies, no one would pay attention to him.

The Man with the Wine

ABOUT FIFTY PEOPLE MADE THEIR WAY along the irregular pathways of the Common, all of them following Alison who stopped at a park bench not far from the great fountain. Two men were seated there, one of them playing guitar, and Matt positioned himself alongside a sheltering tree, close enough to hear the conversation. "It's the bird lady," said the guitar player, and he stopped playing. The other man stared at his feet, at his backpack and sleeping bag.

"Mind your manners, Tom," said the guitarist. "Say hello."

"Don't know her name," said Tom.

Alison sat down and introduced herself.

He stared at Daisy. "That an eagle?"

She told him Daisy's story, adding how intelligent she was.

"She can count to ten, like Big Bird?"

Alison laughed. "She likes music, right, Bill?"

The guitarist plunked a chord. "Not much of a singer, but she gets the beat."

"You play her a song, then," said Tom.

Bill began to play and hum "Yellow Bird." Daisy's head swayed in time to the music.

By then, the line of walkers were circling the bench, standing and sitting and paying attention. Some of them began to hum along to the tune, a song so old that only a few of them could remember the words. Among them were homeless residents of the park who were sitting on the grass, enjoying the warm summer weather, saying hello to some of the parishioners who'd followed Alison.

One woman stood out — Hispanic, Matt thought, her bonnet adorned with ribbons and flowers. She dressed well in what appeared to be Goodwill finery: a loose-fitting yellow dress of Indian cotton, cinched with a gold and orange brocade sash. Nice touch, that sash, he thought. Just as he was wondering if she'd fashioned it out of ancient drapery, he heard a voice, one with the stench of familiarity, a man sitting close to the bench who turned around to address the crowd. "Hey, you guys, look who's here. It's Father Cheapskate, who walks by all the time, and makes like he doesn't see us."

Matt would have cleared out, but he was too close to the front of the group to hide.

"Now don't be rude, friend," said Bill to the man. "We have guests."

The man stood up and glared at Matt. "Well, maybe you can give our guests a little something special, huh?"

Matt felt uncomfortable. Many of the parishioners, fearing confrontation, were beginning to leave.

"I don't want your damned spare change." The man spat the words out.

"Why don't you tell him what you want, then?" asked Bill.

"I know what he wants," said Tom. He looked at the man. "You told me before. You want Father to say Mass."

"That's right! Mass on the grass! How about it?"

Why was I nuts enough to come here? thought Matt. Yet he could not help noticing a murmur of assent from the men and women who lived in the park, who carried their belongings in backpacks and duffel bags, whose faces turned to him, torn with the battle of old shadows and sudden hope. Raw need was something he seldom faced in the eyes of his fortunate parishioners. They were his buffer against these wounded people, and now, they were ebbing away like rinse water down a drain.

"We can't come into the church," said a woman who gestured to her bundle buggy.

"She's right, same goes for us," murmured a chorus.

"Haven't got my gear with me," said Matt. *No vestments, no missal, no bread and wine, cup and plate.*

"Father Matt," said Alison, looking at him intently. She handed him a booklet with the prayers of the Mass.

"See, you got the prayers," said Bill. He raised his old guitar. "And I'm your choir."

Matt wanted to leave.

At that moment, the Hispanic woman made her way forward through the crowd — tall and lean, he realized, with the russet skin and high cheekbones of a Native American. Then she untied her brocade sash, slipped behind him, and draped it over his shoulders.

"Isn't this what the priest wears?" she asked. "Sun and flowers and a bird. Very beautiful."

He realized he would not get away from a man with a plastic bag striding through the crowd with his haul of day-old hamburger buns that some fed-up restaurant owner likely dumped on him, just to get him out of his hair. The man set the full bag down in front of Matt.

I am going to consecrate hamburger buns, he thought.

Then he heard that voice again, like a needle etching a bitter tattoo on his soul.

"Only one thing missing." The garrulous man came forward with a paper bag, the neck of a wine bottle protruding from it.

Just as Matt was about to ask if anyone had a cup, the man with the wine thrust the bottle in his hand, leaned over and whispered in his ear. "Just so you know, I got fucked by a priest. I should spit on you, but I won't. God owes me this Mass."

Shocked, Matt thought it best to ignore him.

"Best wine there is," said the man, and he laughed.

"You need something to drink it from." Another man came forward with a large, unused paper cup. "Swiped it from Starbucks," he said.

Matt never managed to spot the pack rat who set up the battered card table, or the woman who provided the paper plate with the floral design. He poured wine into the cup, placed a hamburger bun on the plate, set the bagful of bread alongside the table. *We don't need candles; we have sunlight.* He gestured for everyone to gather around him. Then, oblivious to stares from passersby, Matt opened Alison's prayer book and began.

Alison later wrote that the air was silent, that even the birds held their breath.

Matt spoke the prayers, read the gospel, then realized he was supposed to preach. He had no thoughts, nothing prepared. He looked out over the crowd. "It's good to be here, celebrating Mass with you," he said. "I should have done it long ago. All of us carry wounds, and some of them refuse to heal. He paused. I am not always sure how to approach you. Forgive me for the ways in which I have not helped you. Pray for me, and I will continue to pray with you."

Matt felt shaken by the wave of anguish and trouble that surrounded him. When he looked up, he noticed that the man who had given him the wine was watching him with a look that was both guarded and alert — unhinged, a broken door pried open by a blade of light.

He reminded himself to be patient.

He prayed over the bread and wine, calling upon the Spirit to bless the gifts, and he thought to himself that only one who understood suffering as Jesus did would think to be present in these unhappy offerings. Yet he felt certain that the goodness in which these humble gifts were given would in some mysterious way transform them.

At Communion time, he broke off a piece of the day-old bread and ate it, chewing the tasteless lump, swallowing in it the misery surrounding him, the suffering ignored — so real that it seemed to hover at the edge of memory, a moment forgotten, a sin of omission on his part, and this troubled him. *As if there were something I lived through and forgot. Something I saw. That close.*

He looked at them as he blessed the cup of wine, and he noticed the hard stare of the man who had given it to him. *The blood of Christ.* He brought the cup to his lips and drank. It was bitter wine, rock-bottom plonk. He saw that the man stood, arms folded, watching him.

He called people forward to receive the bread; most stayed away from the wine. While they filed past, Bill picked up his guitar and played in the background — softly, and rather well, Matt thought. *He must have been a club musician once.* He wondered what sad twist in his life had driven him into the street.

At the end of Mass, it was part of the ritual to consume the remnants of bread and wine, but Matt called over the man who'd given him the bread and returned the outsized bag to him. Likewise, he signalled to the man who had given him the wine, but what remained in the cup was consecrated, and he was supposed to drink it. He wasn't certain he could or should The man took back the bottle, and stood there, watching him.

Matt felt uneasy. "Can I help you with something?" he asked.

"Just drink the wine," answered the man. "Isn't that what the priest does?"

Matt raised the cup to his lips.

"Father used to let me do that in the sacristy after Mass," said the man. "Get me good and hammered, then take me to his room."

"I'm sorry," said Matt.

Your turn now, said the look on his face. "Drink up," he said.

"Excuse me," said a woman's voice.

Alison. She stared at the man.

"Show some respect, John," she said. "Father said the Mass for you. It's not his fault, what happened."

The man looked stunned.

Matt drank the wine and tasted destitution. He drank indignity and suffering, and the bitter taste of innocence lost. He drank the anguish of his own troubled youth.

His throat felt scorched by fire, his body encompassed by a burning warmth that settled into his bones and flesh, then gripped it like a vise, as if holding together a piece of shattered crockery. He could not finish it.

"Don't drink any more," said Alison. "It's no good."

"How would you know that, little lady?" said John.

"By the look on Father's face," she answered.

Matt saw that the man was eyeing him.

"I'll bring the wine again next week," John said.

"You're sure I'm coming?"

"I see it in your face."

"We are required to drink the wine. No matter what it tastes like."

"Don't worry. You'll get used to it."

Matt turned around to see Alison staring at them both. Restless, Daisy rose to her full height and stretched her wings.

"You're taking advantage of his good nature," she said to John.

"It's all right, Alison," said Matt.

"No," said the hammer's clang in her voice. "It is not."

All I Had to Do

I was shocked, Matt wrote a year later, while recovering from his heart attack. *The Mass had forced me to eat the hard bread of life and drink the gall of anguish, to face my own suffering in the mocking eyes of the man with the wine. I had been on drugs, I had killed an innocent soul, and now I found myself among the abused and derelict, and I didn't have to preach a word to them. All I had to do was bless the wine and raise it to my lips, and they could see their own troubles reflected in the look of my distress. Better than some high-and-mighty priest with all the answers, better to be human to the core, but I knew that there was more to this, that I had left some things undone, avoiding pain that inconvenienced me, and so every week through the summer, I said Mass in the Common with the people's humble bread and wine, and I blessed it all, confronting hell, returning from the grave. My soul would have to find a new way to live.*

That, or end up on a park bench. "You will always have to watch out for addiction," *said the doctor.*

And so, I said Mass in the Common. For a while, until I became ill.

137

Ready for Battle

AS MATT WAS ABOUT TO LEAVE, he noticed Alison seated on a park bench, with Daisy on her fist. He went over to join her.

"Do you know these people?" he asked.

"I've spoken to Bill a few times."

He told her he wanted to come back and say Mass for them.

"They want to be outdoors," she said. "They don't feel safe in church."

"You think so?"

Alison turned to look at him, and he saw in her eyes a luminous, steel-edged gaze, the tip of a knife that could pry his heart open. "They feel safe nowhere," she said.

Daisy turned her head to Alison. Matt wasn't sure what to say. Alison's face had changed, its innocence erased by a fierce silence, a feral wariness. He imagined an angel with a flaming sword. "They remind us of our sufferings, don't they," he said.

She turned to look at him. "But that's no reason to let them demean you."

Matt was silent.

"You know how to be good to them," she said. "To say hello. To give change, to say Mass. To eat their wretched bread and drink their wine, to take them into your body." She paused. "But you don't need to be insulted."

Matt had never heard her speak like this. Ready for battle. Joan of Arc in the park, he thought.

Alison stood up, as graceful as a dancer, Daisy sitting tall on her fist. She had recovered her composure, her gentle look, as if the other Alison had been conjured up, imagined by the two of them. She turned away and drifted out of the park, a child as frail and invisible as wind.

The Stain

THE MASS HAD TROUBLED AND MOVED ALISON, and she felt grateful for Father Matt's strength of spirit. In his hands, the act of Communion had drawn out loneliness; in its sign of hope, it had opened wounds. Now, she felt memories leaking out of her, staining her skin like ink from a cheap pen. She feared that if she wrote them down, her soul would be dyed forever with the mark of what had damaged her.

Yet she had to remember. As she received Communion, she swallowed the rough bread of memory, the wine of sorrow. From the looks of the faces surrounding her, everyone had done and felt the same. Somehow, she would find strength in this.

Same As Always

DURING THAT SUMMER, MATT RETURNED to the Common every Sunday to celebrate Mass for the homeless. He came with empty hands, offering whatever bread and wine the people gave him. The man with the wine continued to bring it to the service. The bread was sometimes a baguette, sometimes pita, often a day old. What mattered to Matt was to feel his heart pried open by these gifts.

He lived in fearful camaraderie with lost souls. He prayed for them, and for lonely Alison and wounded Daisy, her companion who would never fly.

After Mass, John always waited, eyeing him while he drank what remained of the wine. "Big cup there," he said. "Good for what ails you."

Matt took that moment to thank him.

"For what?"

"For bringing better wine."

John looked puzzled. "Never. Same as always."

"Doesn't taste the same."

He laughed. "Told you you'd get used to it."

All summer long and into the autumn, he prayed with them, spent time on the park bench listening to Bill's music, watching Tom talk to Daisy the falcon as she clutched Alison's gloved fist, absorbing rough talk and insults from John. "Hey, guys,

Father thought I upgraded the wine, he really likes this plonk now, he said so, right, Father?"

On this particular occasion Matt was growing tired, but he said to John, "The wine's been blessed, it's God's gift," and at that point, Matt had the good sense to leave the park, to return to his living quarters to rest.

It was then that he wondered if he were headed in the right direction. He pondered what his superior might have to say about this as he imagined himself asleep on a park bench, succumbing to bad wine. Alone, he poured himself a Scotch.

Non-Human Guests

THE OUTDOOR MASSES CONTINUED into a mild October, but autumn drew Matt's focus back to the college, stickhandling academic duties, speaking engagements, conference papers, along with weekend parish work. Meanwhile, he'd heard from his old friend Elias who had applied for a teaching position in Boston. "It would begin in a year's time," he wrote. "Natalie's due next month!"

They will never be lonely. The words fell like precious coins — hard, metallic echoes through his body.

He had parish work this weekend for the feast of St. Francis: the annual Blessing of the Animals. Non-human guests would include dogs and cats, caged white mice (courtesy of the choir director's daughter), the Parish Council's president's clutch of pigeons, a rat named Bingo, and, more than likely, one disabled but prayerful peregrine falcon. They had discussed doing the ritual in the Common, but the pastor had said no, people wouldn't bring their pets there. Most didn't share Alison's ease with the residents of the park. "The parishioners are drifting away as it is," Ron said. "Almost none of them come to the outdoors Mass."

That Mass will stop when the weather cools, thought Matt, wondering what he'd do then.

Daisy Might Fuss

ALISON LEFT DAISY'S CAGE IN THE CAR, bore her on her gloved fist and found her way into St. Bartholomew's parking lot, already crowded with other parishioners and their pets. Daisy's reptilian head moved this way and that, her golden eyes aglow at the sight of pigeons, mice, a rat, two ferrets, a couple of hamsters. Alison held tight to Daisy's tethers. "Don't fuss, Daisy," she whispered. "God loves them, too."

Both Father Matt and Father Ron were there to bless each animal, accompanied by altar servers who carried small buckets of holy water. They made their way from pet to pet, sprinkling them, murmuring words of benediction over mutts straining at the leash and restless cats in their containers. Things were going well enough until there came a mighty beating of wings, a horrible thumping sound against a wall of air, and the choir director's daughter screamed because Daisy managed awkward flight from Alison's gloved fist, coming in for a clumsy landing, talons gripping the cage full of mice. Clinging hard, she swung back and forth. The mice crouched in a corner and squealed.

"Daisy!" From her pocket, Alison produced a dead rat, and the falcon returned to the glove for her snack, forgetting the tiny rodents.

"I'm so sorry, everyone," said Alison. "I should have realized that Daisy might fuss."

Daisy nibbled away at the rat, tossing its claws and tail on the ground.

Alison heard a chorus of "Yech.... Gross.... Disgusting."

"You should have realized that Daisy might *snack*," said the pigeon fancier.

The child with the cage of mice began to cry. "She's terrified of your bird," said her mother. "That beak. Those talons."

"Yes, I see," said Alison. She stroked Daisy's head and kissed it, while the mother turned to comfort her daughter.

Then Matt approached her.

"Will you bless Daisy?" she asked him.

Muttering rumbled in her ears, like distant thunder. She watched Matt as he eyed the glares, the unhappy faces. He glanced at the rat bits on the pavement. "Meet me in the sacristy," he said.

Who Her Father Was

MATT WATCHED ALISON AS SHE ENTERED the small room behind the altar, Daisy still on her fist. That creature, so wild and instinctive, seemed to share a kind of moral innocence with its keeper. Alison's eyes held a gaze as astute as the falcon's yet tinged with a puzzlement and sorrow that was hers alone. "Father Matt, I apologize," she said. "I didn't consider the presence of rodents and pigeons." Her voice dropped as she said the words, as if she were afraid that mentioning them might agitate Daisy.

"Well, Daisy is a first for us," said Matt.

"I should have known better. I was afraid of hawks as a child," she said.

"I guess you've had a change of heart."

He could see that Alison was clothed in good intentions, garments that did not snag on the edges of his sarcasm.

"God sent Daisy to help me remember my father."

"Did your dad keep hawks?"

"He was a falconer before I was born. But he had to quit when he came to Canada."

Matt wondered if there was some Canadian law against falconry.

"He had to focus on a whole new life," she said.

She makes him sound like a convict on the run, Matt thought.

"He didn't want to go to Vietnam."

Matt could feel his silence thicken the air. *Her father would have been my age.*

"Will you bless Daisy?" she said at last.

Matt made the sign of the cross over the falcon and recited the prayer:

"Lord God, we ask you to bless Daisy. By the power of your love, enable her to live according to your plan. May we always praise you for all your beauty in creation. Blessed are you, Lord our God, in all your creatures! Amen."

Matt sprinkled holy water over Daisy's head. She lifted her eyes to look at him.

"Thank you for being so kind to her," said Alison.

"You have an unusual vocation," he replied.

"I appreciate you saying that," she said. She explained that only her colleagues who worked with wild birds understood the depth of her attachment to Daisy.

"I'm saying that you have a strong spiritual sense," he continued.

"Well…" She looked away.

"I don't mean to embarrass you, but it's a gift from God that we don't see often."

"Daisy is part of the gift. She's almost my spiritual director."

Matt had never heard anyone talk like this. Taking direction from a bird of prey, from Daisy the rodent-slayer. He found it sad that such a bright young woman, so apparently devout, seemed to know so little about the richness of her own faith-tradition. Yet he thought of his own youth, how ill-equipped he was to handle a spiritual crisis.

Her father fled the war. I didn't have the courage to do that.

Years later, the least he could do was to offer guidance to someone whose strong moral sense came from a man far braver than himself.

"I don't want to push this," he said. "But have you ever

thought of religious life? It gives wonderful formation, good companionship, constant spiritual direction."

"They'd never take Daisy."

"True enough."

"I suspect that I'm meant to be a hermit," she said.

"Have you no family?" he asked her.

"My mom's in Montreal." She seemed indifferent to her own words, as if they were lint she was picking off her sleeve.

"Try to pray about it, Alison," he said to her. "It's never good to be too alone."

"I'm glad I have Daisy."

"Your mother only has you. She may be lonely with your father gone."

"She's with her boyfriend. Not Lucien, but someone else." She spoke as if Matt weren't there, as if she were talking to herself. Or to God.

She isn't living in the real world.

Earth to Alison. Over and out.

Alison's visit troubled him. She seemed eccentric, but not ill; engaged in an inner dialogue, one she'd let escape into sound and language, like a clumsy kid who's yanked the earbuds out of her smart phone and sent a flood of rock music into the street. *Perhaps she's talking to her father.*

From Alison's Journal

The incident at the animal blessing was my own fault. I apologized to Mrs. Malley, whose daughter was so frightened of Daisy, but she just told me that birds of prey had no place around children. I had a lot of explaining to do, since I believe that Daisy is also one of God's children, and, with her imperfect wing, one of the least of these, as the Gospel says. Yet nothing excuses the fact that I'd forgotten my childhood, how frightened I had once been by a hawk. The circumstances were not the same, it's true. Yet even more true is the fact that I longed to forget what happened. Maybe I will, once I have written the whole thing down.

Alison

When I Was Afraid of Hawks

BOSTON, OCTOBER 5, 2010

I remember that I was about to turn eight years old, and my mother, small and quick as a kestrel in flight, was taking off with her colleague Lucien for a photo shoot in Quebec. She was going to miss my birthday, and knowing this, I wept.

"Sweetheart, don't cry," she said. "When I come back, we'll have a big party."

Dad didn't try to stop Mom. Instead he promised to take me birding for my birthday. He pulled out his handkerchief and dried my eyes.

He loved to sit with me, sharing his books full of grand, extravagant birds of prey — the peregrine, the great horned owl, the red-tailed hawk. Having once been a falconer, he still yearned to fly these sparks of light, and he would speak to me with joy about each of these magnificent birds, but I would see only talons and claws, and feel the blood, the torn flesh of absence, numb with disappointment at my mother's indifference.

Yet because of her flight, I wanted to be close to my father, I wanted to fly to retrieve her, and so I sat with him and gazed at the raptors, the circle of light they drew around my one loving parent, so that the fierce enormity of these creatures didn't matter. What mattered was that in my father's generous

153

heart, there was room for myself and the great hawks both. "Haggards," he called the grown-up hawks, their special name. He talked to me about them, compared them to tiny songbirds, showed me pictures of red-tailed hawks, how tender they were as they fed their chicks.

    "A hawk chick is called an 'eyas,'" he said.

    Why?"

    "I don't know, sweetheart. It's just an old word."

Eyas. The fluffy hawklets had a name all their own, which meant they were beloved creatures, and so I let the word loose in my mind as I reached out and touched the baby bird on the page. I imagined that I was smoothing the feathers of the mother hawk, patting the little ones, and then I closed my eyes and slipped underneath the haggard's wing — as if I, too, were an eyas, gifted with a special name, a slight creature of wind and air, helpless, not yet able to fly.

On my eighth birthday, we drove to a beautiful location, Golden Willow Conservation Area, just a ten-minute drive north of Toronto. "Raptor Experience," said the sign, and I imagined a nest, a great mother hawk, her pale breast feathers tipped with amber light, and her tiny eyasses, mouths open, waiting for her to feed them. I was going to see this. Experience it. What I did not see was the look of consternation on the guide's face. "She knows a lot about birds," Dad said to the guide. "She's very mature for her age."

    At the edge of a field, there were several raptors, tethered and placed on pedestals: identified as a peregrine falcon, a red-tailed hawk, a harrier, and a kestrel. "These are birds of prey," explained the guide. "For centuries, men have trained them to hunt, and our birds are also trained to hunt for you. And they will come to you for food."

I looked around, but saw no nests.

Flying the birds was only for those with prior experience in falconry. "Are there any falconers here?" asked the guide. My father's eyes flashed blue fire. He raised his hand.

I watched. She'll fly to a nest, *said my nerves, my bones.*

On his gloved fist sat an enormous red-tailed hawk named Princess. When he removed her hood, I could see that she had dark eyes, sunlight etching her brown wing feathers, a proud and regal stance. She doesn't like me, *I thought.*

I watched my dad, his hands alive to the memory of the falcon he'd once trained as he learned again how to hold, attach, and release the tethers. He seemed not to notice me, to be in awe of Princess, to be as still as a rabbit about to be devoured.

Then he let Princess go free. A rustle of feathers, an extraordinary flapping of dappled wings, the spread of her great red tail, and with a jingling of her tiny bell, she glided away, soaring above the treetops.

"Is she going to her nest?" I asked.

"She's going to hunt," he said.

"I want to see her nest," I whispered.

My dad did not respond. He was rapt, attending to the hawk, as if Princess were all that mattered to him.

I watched with disappointment as the great hawk circled the sky, as one or two other participants released their birds. It was too much for me, this huge hawk eclipsing the sun, casting its shadow on my father; incoming hawks and falcons swooping overhead, returning to their falconers.

"Way to go, Princess!" Dad said.

"When are we going to see her nest?"

"She hasn't got a nest."

But that's what I wanted to see. I was close to tears. It was my birthday after all, and so I glanced at the enormous hawk who now seemed a monstrous creature, cruel and dangerous. At the sound of her name, she came soaring toward Dad's glove with a confident beating and folding of her enormous wings, casting light into shadow all around her. In her huge talons, she was carrying the ripped and bloodied carcass of a dead squirrel. The poor thing — its stomach torn open, its entrails dangling like disgusting little red balloons.

Smacked with a wave of nausea, I threw up.

This was supposed to be a special treat, and I had hoped to see hawk babies. Instead, horrible Princess went and killed a squirrel and made me sick to my stomach.

This is how I tell the story now, knowing that I was much too young to put words to all of my complicated feelings. It felt as if the earth itself had stopped breathing. I couldn't comprehend Princess, her strange, enormous eyes, the sharp curve of her beak and her talons clutching prey, the commanding stance of her broad wings and tail — it was too fearsome, far too strange for me. I'd wanted to see a nest, to look at the fluffy eyasses, warmed by the comfort of a red-tailed hawk, her large and generous body.

There wasn't any comfort to be had.

I threw up some more and I wept.

My father had to clean me up and apologize to everyone. I can remember how upset the adults looked, except for a woman who knelt down beside me, put an arm around me and dried my eyes. "Don't be afraid, honey," she said, casting a glance at my dad, which I knew even then meant, "What kind of idiot brings an eight-year-old to a falconry run?" Yet I felt sure they were angry at me — a big girl, throwing up and crying like that. I felt ashamed, yet I couldn't help myself. It was my birthday. The big hawk didn't have babies. She was a savage killer and she was going to hurt me, too.

The guide approached us. "I'm going to have to ask you to

leave," he said to my dad. "She's really too young to understand this, and it's upsetting the others."

My father apologized again for my behaviour. As we were leaving, I overheard one guide speaking to another. "Just a poor little kid scared of the hawk."

I started crying again.

In the car, Dad told me he was sorry I'd been scared. "Honey, she wouldn't hurt you."

"I wanted to see her nest. I thought we were going to see the eyasses. Like in the book."

My dad was silent for a moment. "I should have told you," he said at last. "She doesn't have a nest, hon. She's a special bird."

"All birds have nests."

"I guess you're disappointed," he said at last.

I told him the hawks were too big, that I only liked small birds.

"Maybe when you're older," he said.

"No. Only small birds."

On the way home, Dad tried to explain that Princess was bred in captivity, that she didn't need a nest, that she had her own special beauty.

"She scared me. She's a mean hawk and I hate her. I don't care."

Think of the Sound

From: alison@sbas.com
To: cameraman@fordhamu.edu
Re: Animal blessing
Date: Oct. 6, 2010

Hi Cam,
Have you ever attended an animal blessing? I brought Daisy
to ours, and she jumped on a little girl's mouse cage, flapping
her wings and upsetting the child. What a mistake. I distracted
Daisy by waving a dead rat at her, and she flew back to me,
but I upset all the parishioners, including Fr. Matt. I should
have known better. I was afraid of hawks as a kid. I have been
writing about this.
No need to rush with a reply. Hope all's well at Fordham.
Alison

From: cameraman@fordhamu.edu
To: alison@sbas.com
Re: Animal blessing
Date: Oct. 6, 2010

Whatever Daisy did, be sure that she is blessed, no matter what.
No harm was done. I've been to animal blessings and sometimes
the critters behave and sometimes they don't. God loves them

just the way they are. Alison, I would not have guessed that you were ever afraid of hawks.
Cam

From: alison@sbas.com
To: cameraman@fordhamu.edu
Re: Animal blessing
Date: Oct. 6, 2010

Yes, I was scared. My dad took me to a Raptor Experience when I was eight. He loved falconry. His hawk butchered a squirrel and I got upset. Poor dad never flew a hawk again and then he left us.
Alison

From: cameraman@fordhamu.edu
To: alison@sbas.com
Re: Animal blessing
Date: Oct. 6, 2010

Alison, I'm sure your father felt badly about your fear, but I would not assume that he never flew a hawk again because of it. I hope you are at peace with that. I realize that he is not alive now, and that the death of a parent is a profound matter, not to be spoken of with casual words.
Cam

From: alison@sbas.com
To: cameraman@fordhamu.edu
Re: Animal blessing
Date: Oct. 12, 2010

It was a mystery, how and why he died. And it's true, there are no words for the impact of a parent's death when you are still a child. You have to think in terms of sounds, not words. How I felt — think of the sound that a Barn Owl makes, a scream that is close to strangulation.

Alison

What Alison Kept to Herself

My father loved them so much, the hawks and falcons. He believed that he could communicate with them, that they understood more than we realized. He told this to my mother, who found it intriguing, who'd become a prominent photojournalist. She loved venturing into the wilderness, and she would bring back magnificent shots of bald eagles, goshawks, rough-legged hawks, and falcons. He was so grateful for all that beauty. He framed and hung the pictures in his office, while my mother went off on assignment with her colleague Lucien, from Radio-Canada.

Dad didn't seem to mind her absences. He never seemed lonely.

It would not have occurred to me that anything was amiss. Except that I missed my mother.

"Can't you make her stay home?" I asked.

"Your mother takes beautiful pictures," he said.

"But I want her home."

"I know," he told me. "But adults sometimes have to leave home. When you get older, you'll understand."

"I'm going to pray that she'll stay home."

My father looked sad.

"Just pray for your mother's happiness," he said.

As time went on, I sensed that there was a tacit arrangement

161

between my parents, a pact of silence made to adapt to a thing that could never change. My mother and father seemed to be friends. Yet I came to realize that they had parted, as a river forks in the wilderness, each branch meandering through gnarled and craggy hillsides, separate and distant. Perhaps they stayed married because they complemented each other; she an adventurer, he a monkish, retiring man, each made more alive by the tug and pull of the other's vagrant life, the tantalizing image of who they were not.

Or perhaps each needed an adversary, against whom they could pride themselves.

They did not stay married because of me. Of that I am certain.

Dad's friend Edward often came to visit on weekends while Mom was away. He was younger, a doctoral student, and in mild weather, the two men would sit on the front porch, enjoying a beer and grownup conversation. Saturday evenings, they would go for a walk and a movie, and through my parents' prior arrangement, I'd be invited to sleep over at a friend's. When I'd return the following morning, Edward would still be there, having breakfast with Dad.

In time my father retreated to his solitary cabin near Lake Simcoe, where he read and prayed and nurtured his passionate dream of flying the hawks, of seeing through their eyes into the soul of humankind while my mother began to drift away into the ineffable light of the camera's eye, and into the open heart of Lucien.

Dad had his work and he had Edward. Nothing more was said, and life went on.

Yet after the hawk incident on my birthday, I felt that I had injured my father. He was as kind as ever, but it seemed to me that under pale skin, he was raw to the bone, lit from inside in a troubling way, as if the memory of Princess had stirred to life a part of him he'd abandoned, the dreamer who'd had to stop dreaming of soaring birds in the face of real flight as a refugee. He seemed grief-stricken, and for the longest time, I thought it was my fault, that I'd disappointed him because I didn't like Princess.

Only now do I understand that what he touched that day in the park was as sorrowful as my own disappointment. He was not elated by the hawk's magnificence after all. In her flight, he understood what he had lost, as in her flight I understood what I would never find. Yet I didn't know this. I only knew that my father was distressed.

My mother continued to come and go on her photo assignments, and then one weekend, I noticed that Dad's friend Edward no longer came to visit us. I wondered what had become of him, and I told my dad that I missed him.

"Don't worry, honey," he said. "He'll be fine."

"Will he be back?"

"When I see him," said my dad, "I'll tell him you miss him."

Yet I had the feeling he'd do no such thing. I felt a certain remoteness in my dad, as if after he'd flown the hawk, everything familiar had been altered somehow, his hold on this earth dissolved, even kind Edward gone to dust, quite incapable of coming back, of knowing that I missed him.

My father wanted to fly with the hawks and could not while my mother, who'd wanted another kind of life, had seized it and left us. That was the truth; I knew it even then.

My father took to spending weekends up north in his cabin on Lake Simcoe, "his retreat-house," my mother called it. I'd only been inside the cabin once or twice when Dad took me swimming up at the lake. The dwelling was quite small; a table and two chairs, crowded bookshelves, a pot-bellied stove, a couch that served as a bed. On one wall, a crucifix, a rosary looped over it.

When Dad left for the cabin, he'd no longer ask me to come. I'd stay with the neighbours if Mom was on assignment. On his way home from the lake, Dad would usually stop by to pick me up, but on one of these autumn weekends, it was my mother who came to get me. The neighbours had called my house since it was suppertime and growing late. It was fortunate that my mother was home. "I don't know where your father is," said my mom. "There must have been traffic on the 400."

My dad never returned. He was found dead in his northern cabin, burrowing in a cave of blankets like a wounded bear, asleep with the woodstove on, windows shut, surrounded by his books on nature and philosophy. "An accident," said the coroner. "Tired from a hike and he just wasn't thinking."

"He fell asleep and forgot to open the window," said my mother. I wept. Even then, I feared that my father had suffered one too many devastating losses, that the terrible rock-weight of life had toppled down and crushed him. He'd had to flee his country, my mother didn't love him, something had happened to Edward. He couldn't even become a falconer because I was afraid of hawks, and it was my fault that the last blow had struck him.

I was inconsolable with grief. At the funeral, the priest spoke about his gentleness, his love of nature, how he had given this gift to his little daughter and to the many students he had taught. It was the only moment of comfort that I felt, along with the words of Sister Marie at school. She told me my father had flown to heaven with the birds, and that made me cry. She gave me a book of prayers to say. She was very kind.

Perhaps it was only natural that such a quiet soul would die in his sleep. I like to think that he died a gentle death, that he faded in brightness, like the brilliant colours of a painting when exposed to too much sunlight.

Yet, I have lived haunted by that birthday in the park when I wanted a nest and instead was frightened by the beating wings and talons of a great hawk, how I cried in grief and disappointment over a loss beyond my capacity to name, when I disrupted the group and had to be sent home. Only now do I understand that my father had wanted me to bear witness to a joy he could not experience. He never again tried to fly a hawk or falcon. It was as if at that very moment, he began to leave this world.

Waiting for the Rain

BOSTON, OCTOBER 6, 2010

When I lost my dad, I did not recognize my loneliness, how it hollowed me out like a fierce wind, as if I were living in Toronto's ravines, exposed to the elements, adapted to the wild. I imagined myself a hawk, a squirrel, a fox, a rat — both predator and prey. Eight years passed, but my sorrow did not. I no longer wanted to be human, with all of its attendant sufferings. My mother abandoned Lucien, who wanted to marry her. Then Wendell moved in, with his lion's mane of hair and dove-grey eyes, a brotherly casualness full of open spaces, prairie solitude, cloudless morning skies. He was kind to me; he peered into my heart, cupped my spirit in the warmth of his hands like a baby bird that had fallen from its nest, and I felt enticed. My mouth dry, my soul a desert waiting for rain, until my mother was away and one night Wendell slipped into my bed and I was lonely and he said to me, "I'm fond of you, Alison." He kissed me, slipped off my clothes, told me how much he loved my silken hair, stroked and caressed it. Afterwards, he said, "Dear Alison, everyone has a first time. Better it happens at home, with someone you trust," and so it happened. And it happened again, and I became wild, a creature of the forest, thinking nothing of what I was doing, what had been done to me. I will tell no one any of this.

Wendell

ALISON LEFT OUT MORE THAN THIS from the memories she recorded, and from the terse emails she'd send to Cameron Byrne. And so, she began to disturb the impacted soil of her life like a robin yanking out worms, unaware of how much living matter lay buried in the deep earth, how one tale was tangled with another.

She recalled that in 2003 — eight years after her father's death — her mother left Toronto in order to flee what she considered an odious betrayal by her daughter. She sold their midtown condo at Bloor and Castle Frank, uprooted Wendell, and moved with him to Montreal, leaving Alison money for expenses and the rent of a small apartment.

While Alison was alone and preparing to leave, Wendell returned to say goodbye. Upset, she said to him, "Why did you do that to me?

And he said, "Do what?"

She started to cry. "You got me in trouble with my mom," she said, but he apologized, saying that he meant no harm, that he cared for her.

And then he grabbed her shoulders, pressed her against the wall, his hand stroking her long, lustrous hair and he tried to kiss her, but she pushed him away.

"Tiger, I love that silky coat of yours," he whispered. "Let's keep in touch." He gave her his card with his cellphone number. "I'll be in and out of Toronto. Send me your number and your new address."

Alison was crying. He made her insides tremble, like wet leaves in a storm.

He tried again, kissed her hard, then left.

She went into the kitchen, found scissors, headed for her mother's room, stood in front of the full-length mirror and cut off her hair. "*'Tiger, I love that silky coat of yours.'* Well, fuck you," she said, as she kept cutting, letting her tresses fall to the floor like a hunted beast struck dead, as if she were casting off both innocence and its destruction. She felt herself growing as feral as a wildcat, her hair becoming boyish, spiky and unkempt, like a comic-book version of a crown of thorns.

Like Her Father

DAD WOULD BE UPSET AT MY LANGUAGE, Alison thought. *He would be ashamed of me.* She'd felt pained by these thoughts of disapproval from someone she'd loved. Looking back, she now recalled how obsessed she'd been at the age of eighteen by the spirit of her father, having no other adult to whom she could turn. She remembered how he would walk her through the Nordheimer Ravine running south off St. Clair, how he would show her the wildlife in the Brickworks and the Humber ravine, Rosedale Valley, and Mimico Creek. At night, she dreamt that he led her into the woods in order to show her the poor shack by a distant lake where his life came to an end. "I'll show you the way home," he said to her. "Give me your hand, and I'll take you there."

When she awoke, she decided to cleanse herself of all that had happened, to follow the woodland paths that her father had shown her, to let him be with her in spirit. She would gather her camping gear, take the subway, return to the trails of her west-end childhood, then find her way eastward to Rosedale Valley Road and south into the ravines along the Don River. She would be close to midtown, the library, the bank, and there she would live in solitude until she had recovered from the fever that had seized her.

The time would come when she would belong to the woods, when cold and hunger would whittle her bones, trimming

169

away the flesh of longing. She would spend part of every day in meditation as her father did. In her backpack, she stuffed his crucifix and prayer book, objects from his wilderness cabin that bore witness to the death of autumn and spring's return, and to the homeward flight of the birds.

Or perhaps, like her father, she would hide her wounds, lie down in her sleeping bag, homeless under the stars, go to sleep, and never wake up.

Stranger

LUGGING HER BACKPACK, ALISON WALKED to the Castle Frank subway stop, across the Bloor Viaduct that arched across the Don Valley, up and down, up and down, like a great metal Slinky-toy, frozen into place. City officials had woven a metallic veil along the sides of the bridge to prevent troubled people from hurling themselves downward. She could not end her life here.

She wiped away tears. *Besides, I'm a coward.*

No. I feel ashamed.

I'm here to face that feeling of shame, not to throw myself off a bridge.

Although doing one seemed to invite the other.

She stood on the westbound platform at Castle Frank, positioning herself at the east end where the subway train entered the tunnel, its lights shining like the luminous eyes of an owl in the dark, and she leaned against the wall, knowing that otherwise she would have been drawn to the refuge of the subway tracks because she couldn't rid herself of the touch of a man whom she'd allowed to poison her, who'd made her feel so ashamed, who'd played with her loneliness and still would, if she let him.

"The only way to get rid of the sufferings of the body," her father wrote, "is through stillness, isolation, prayer. I want to go back to the elements, to bury what I feel and long for." A note her mother found in his possessions.

He did not mention suicide. His death was an accident.

More than anything, she wanted to do what he had done.

She was not homeless. The earth was her home, as it had been for her father.

Standing on the platform at Castle Frank was a man who looked like her dad. He would have been the same age, his gaze both remote and kindly, and she felt for a moment that her father's spirit had come to walk with her, to save her from destruction. The university was three or four stops west, and she assumed that the man was a professor because he dressed for work with the same inattention as her father once did, in not-quite-matching shirt and slacks, rumpled jacket and tie. He even wore the same preoccupied look, as if he were mulling over his lecture notes. I bet he teaches on campus, she thought. *He's probably off to a class.*

When the man got off at St. George, she did, too, following him and a crowd of backpacking students traipsing upstairs to the University line. Most — including the man — boarded the southbound train and got off at the Museum stop; she did the same, walking down the west side of Queens Park Crescent, heading south toward Hoskin Avenue, close to Trinity College. *Wonder if he teaches there.* Across the way from the Anglican chapel was Hart House, august and formal, host to a conference of some kind. Academics, men in suits and ties, women in dresses and heels were milling around the entrance to the hall. The man was headed in the same direction. Alison realized that she was about to lose him because she couldn't pass through a mob of people with her enormous backpack.

"I don't know what I'm doing here," she said aloud. She could feel the tears in her voice.

The man stopped, turned around. "Are you lost?" he asked her.

"Yes," she said, because his simple question struck her to the depths.

"Where are you trying to go?"

"Home," she said, not knowing where that was.

"Where is home?"

Oh God, if I only knew. She wished for the courage to speak this thought but she could not find it. Yet something about this man touched her. He seemed like a minister or a priest — which word did Anglicans use? She wasn't sure. No, he was neither. He seemed like the spirit of her father.

"I need to get to St. Clair and Spadina," she replied. She knew the way, but she wanted to provide him with a sensible answer, since he was kind enough to speak to her. She had planned to go there, get off and walk east to Sir Winston Churchill Park, and then down into the ravine, where she would camp for the night.

The man eyed her. "Go back to the St. George subway entrance and take the Bloor train west to Spadina," he said. "Then transfer and go north to St. Clair." He paused. "Do you need a token?" he asked.

"Yes," she replied, even though she didn't, because she figured she had better learn to scrounge, even beg. The day might come when she'd need a fare and have no money to buy it. More than that, she understood herself to be a pilgrim, and to receive the token was to acknowledge her need for help, her willingness to receive it.

Yet kindness fled the man's eyes like a dull sun fading into ragged cloud; pity tinged with fear clung to his tightened lips as he dug into his pocket, pulled out a token, gave it to her, and then handed her a toonie. "Get yourself a coffee," he said. She thanked him, then asked him if he taught here.

"Now and then," he said. Then turned his back and was lost in the crowd.

Alison's face stung, as if slapped. Through his eyes, she was a street kid, not a pilgrim. Someone who might do him harm.

He sees right through me, she thought, and he knows what I've done.

"Well, what would you expect?" Her mother's voice. "It's your own fault."

Fair enough, I guess. But I'm going to make up for it.

She made her way to the subway station. Near the Bedford entrance sat a man wrapped in blankets, a small pile of newspapers and a large dog seated beside him. The man was jingling a cupful of coins. She dropped the toonie in his cup, looked him in the eye as she did it, and said, "Good day."

"Would you like something to read?" he asked. She nodded, and he handed her a copy of *The Varsity*. Then she went into the subway.

The Last Day

YEARS LATER, THE ADULT ALISON remembered Toronto as a city haunted by a profound silence. This is how her father would describe it when he took her walking in its ravines, the weave of green spaces threaded by rivers, almost all of which were buried or vanished. Only she would not treasure those ravine walks now. It would become a torment to think of them, but Alison didn't know that at the time the professor embarrassed her.

She'd used his token to make her way west by subway and then north, getting off at the St. Clair station, walking to the corner of Wells Hill Avenue and down the flight of steps descending into the Nordheimer Ravine. She had grown up not far from here, on a modest street near St. Clair and Oakwood, and it seemed to her that she might find solace in a place where she'd once walked in innocence.

Down the steep hillside of stairs she went, feeling as weightless as a falling leaf, as if entry into this space altered gravity and swallowed the city whole. The roar of cars along St. Clair softened to a distant humming. Everything became still, as in the moments before sleep.

She could hide here. Toronto had a deep soul, her father used to say — a hidden place within itself, and this silence was its primal state, interrupted by the clumsy missteps of the city's morning traffic, then subsiding into rest. She felt comforted, walking through the fragile latticework of maple, cottonwood, ash, and oak, the mottled light of afternoon sifting through treetops to the path below as she passed dog-walkers and cyclists on the trail.

As she approached St. Clair Brook, she imagined it a creature as lost as she was, and then she glanced upward at the steep inclines, recalling that high above were houses, human aeries, lookouts. A wealthy neighbourhood. She would not be allowed to pitch a tent here; she'd have to keep moving.

Yet she felt exhausted. She sat down, leaned against a maple tree, and fell asleep. She dreamt that its blood-red leaves fell down and buried her.

When she woke up from her nap, she decided to find her way to the Don Valley Ravine, further east. It was a spot where she'd seen encampments, but there were none allowed in this place of comfort. The east end of town, she thought, would be better. Bare and impoverished, nothing to distract her from restoring her life through prayer and meditation. Then she realized that what she'd imagined might be dangerous. She'd brought no self-protection, no knives or pepper spray. Insect repellent, yes, she remembered that. *What would I do if someone stole my camping gear?* She'd tucked her money into her underwear. Without it, she'd end up panhandling, turning tricks. Then she would die.

Oh God, have mercy. Hold me in the shadow of your wings.

She would be all right. She felt safer outdoors, far from the closeted nightmare of Wendell and her desire for him. If she was meant to live, she would.

Alison trudged toward Davenport Road and under the train tracks to Dupont. Passing a food market, she bought a sack of peanuts in their shells and stuffed it into her backpack. *Looking after the squirrels. It's something to do with my time.* At Dupont, she boarded the subway, went south, then travelled east to Castle Frank where she'd first boarded the train that day. There, she got off and made a detour through the ravine lands near Rosedale Valley Road. A beautiful day, another lovely neighbourhood, as she entered the seclusion of the city's forest, sharing the wooded paths with joggers and cyclists.

Today is the last day that I'm one of them, she thought. *In a few weeks' time, they won't even notice me. I'll be sleeping under a tarp, a lump just off the path. But not here. Where I'm going, they'll never come.* At this point, she didn't care where she ended up. She felt exhausted, as if she might evaporate like a puddle of water in sunlight. She didn't want anyone to see her.

She found a park bench, snacked on an apple, dozed for a few minutes, then headed east, and south of the Bloor Viaduct.

Tired, she inched her way through the undergrowth, out of sight of the walking paths, until she caught a glint of dark water needled with shards of light, the Don River. "Once serpentine, once considered as filth, a toxic brew," said her father. "Its banks became home," he would say, "to the city's less fortunate." A broken river, one forced by the nineteenth century into a straight path, a reform measure for the vagaries of nature in a growing city. The poor, fetid thing, poisoned, blamed for the spread of illness, bent into what the city fathers thought of as a pleasing, uniform shape. The Parks and Rec people were trying to coax the Don back into life with plantings and landscape, walking trails, and proper garbage bins. That, Alison feared, would mean the end of its encampments, of those who could not bear to be indoors, who found hope in solitude, in fierce independence, in the wilderness of earth and sky.

This world would not make an end of her. She meant to live in the forest, close to the earth.

She entered an underpass, its bare concrete taunted by graffiti, glimpsing beyond it a makeshift encampment. Scattered about were a few tents, an assortment of cooking utensils, plastic bags, old tarps, empty bottles of wine. It made her wary, afraid. "You have to do this," said her father's voice. "You have to pray in the dark."

You have to live with what you did, she thought. *Until it dies in you.*

What she had done was reflected in the bleakness of the place. She didn't have to be here. Her mother had left her funds enough to rent a room, at least. The money was in the bank, in her own account. Yet whenever she thought of being indoors, she'd feel Wendell's touch and start to cry.

"I'm afraid to live indoors," she whispered.

"It's all right," said her father's voice. "I'm here."

Where was the sound coming from? *Maybe I'm losing my mind. If you think you're nuts, you probably aren't.*

I'd rather beg than take money from Mom, she thought.

You Must Care

ALISON FELT AS FRAIL AS AN OLD LEAF, her old life drifting away. Too brittle for thought, a dead patch of colour that would crumble underfoot. *Under whose foot?* She didn't care.

"You must care."

She heard her father's voice in the clearing beyond the underpass, felt his hand on hers because this was his abode, and he walked her to a wooded grove, a space that seemed to open up in sight of the river where she could pitch her tent. "There's no one here right now," he said. "Settle in."

"What shall I do now," she whispered once the tent was up, and his voice said, "Pray for your life." She dug into her backpack, pulled out her father's crucifix, and hooked the cross on a strut inside the tent flap. Then she knelt, closed her eyes in exhaustion, and murmured one of her father's prayers as if she were talking in her sleep. *"May I shelter in the shadow of your wings, oh God."*

Moments later, she grew alert to the crunch of footsteps, twigs snapping under their weight.

"What do we have here?" A man's voice.

"Christ, another Jesus-nut."

"Like crazy Annie." Another man.

"Where'd she go, crazy Annie?"

"Down the fucking drain, from booze."

The voices dropped to a whisper.

"Shit. Just a kid."

Alison felt too tired to reply. She was doing this not out of piety, but because her father had told her how to save herself. A crazy kid, raw with the need to wrench her life from the grip of memory, as if praying would peel away Wendell's touch, leaving only the stinging pain of regret.

"Why did I do that?" she asked God. "Tell me why I did that."

He'd made her pregnant. Her mother took her to the doctor. Rage like a meat hook, digging at her insides.

She made the sign of the cross, then peered outside the tent. A crowd of men and women were gazing at her. Some of them were bedraggled, some of them smelled of alcohol and darkness. Curiosity, amazement, even a kind of rough tenderness — she felt all of this. Yet she did not feel inclined to talk to anyone.

"You pray for us?" a voice said.

"If you like, I will."

"You heal the sick'n stuff like that?"

"No, no," she said. "I'm here to pray, that's all."

"How come?" a man asked.

"I need help. My father tells me, 'pray.'"

"There's a church up the road, girlie."

"I don't want to go indoors."

Murmurs of assent.

"How old are you, child?" asked a woman.

"Eighteen."

"You need anything, you speak up," said a bearded man who took a swig from a hip flask, then waved it in her direction.

"Your father know you're here?" a woman asked.

"My father's dead. But yes, he knows. He talks to me."

"Poor soul," she heard someone whisper.

Yet she had felt his hand guiding her away from the bridge and the subway tracks, and he had, for a moment, opened the heart of a man kind enough to ask her where her home was.

And look, she was safe here with fellow drifters. She would lift her eyes to the trees where the birds would nest in spring, if she lived that long.

The Owl

ALISON WAS SWEATING MEMORIES, And the pores of her body wept. All those years ago, and I can't shake it, she thought.

The falcon turned her head toward her, great eyes wide, as if to say, "Shake what?"

Alison kissed Daisy's head, then dried her eyes, remembering how she awoke that first night in the ravine to hear an owl's soft hooting. *Hoo-h'HOO-hoo-hoo*. She crawled out of her sleeping bag, opened the tent flap, and peered outside. The brilliant disk of the moon dangled above her, an ornament piercing the night's skin, and high up in a thicket of trees facing her tent, she heard the sound again, then saw, silhouetted against the moon, an enormous great horned owl. A golden-eyed creature with large, tufted ears, its fierce talons locked on a branch, a night hunter in search of prey. There must be plenty of food in the ravine, she thought. *Mice and voles*. She thought of that sack of peanuts in the tent, something the mice would appreciate as they scurried among the leaves in search of food. Watching the owl, she felt its eyes connect with hers. *Won't go hungry. Lots to eat here*. The owl flew away.

Alison reached for a peanut in its shell and placed it on the ground near her tent. Before long, she saw a grey-furred form, the gleam of obsidian eyes, tiny claws, a scaly, pink tail. *Eat*, she thought. *You are not long for this world*. The rat scurried off with the nut. A few moments later, she heard it rustling the leaves. She put another nut in the palm of her hand, then let it roll to the ground. *Take it and eat, poor thing. You're here to feed the owl.*

She saw no reason not to feed the rats — creatures so lowly and despised.

The rodent gripped the nut and ran.

Bitter Wine

ALISON BECAME AWARE THAT HER COMPANIONS thought she was crazy. Sometimes she talked out loud to herself, mentioning the owl, offering food to the squirrels that gathered near her tent. *They've never been close to nature, that's why they think I'm crazy.* Yet she was also aware that both her youth and her strangeness protected her, as if she possessed a kind of innocence that the others admired.

At the end of the day, people would gather outside her tent for evening prayers. They seemed to find some consolation in the gentle sound of her voice because they began to write out their intentions, scribbled in pencil by shaking hands on the backs of government envelopes that once held social assistance cheques, and they would ask her to read them out loud. "Let us pray for Frank, that he will find work; let us pray for Bob, that he'll receive the money stolen from his tent; let us pray for Frieda, that her children will take her in," and everyone would murmur, "Lord, hear our prayer," because one or two of them had been Catholics once and through the dimming pathways of memory, that old response meandered until it found its way to their lips. The others copied them.

Afterwards, they would scatter, returning to their tents and bedrolls, but one evening Frieda said, "Why don't we share a nightcap," and she pulled out a bottle and some paper cups she'd filched from a library washroom, filled them, and passed them around. Alison took a cup. She wasn't used to drinking, and she didn't like whatever it was, but she didn't want to look like a snob, so she swigged it down, as the others did. It tasted terrible.

"Sweet Miss Innocence drinks like a sailor, well fucking shit," said Frieda. She held out the bottle. "Come on, sweetheart, drink up."

Alison shook her head, no.

"Whisper sweet prayers into my ear. Come and warm up my bed."

"Get lost, Frieda," said Mike.

"I'm in love with Alison," said Frieda as she wandered off.

"Ignore that old whore," said Charlie.

"I thought Frieda had kids," Alison said.

"Two. Doesn't know who the fathers are. Too ugly now to turn tricks."

Alison returned to her tent and closed the flap. She had to find a way to make the best of this. She had chosen to live here, after all.

Meat Locker

ALISON TRIED TO GIVE SHAPE TO HER NEW LIFE. Yet it seemed that she lived under an enormous wave of gravity, a force that was pulling her skin into shapelessness, tugging at her fragile bones until they felt ready to break. It was the place, the ravine, the encampment. It did not enjoy the rules of time or the clarity of space; it forced her to enter the wilderness of her body, to disassemble everything, to be restored to wholeness. Yet she'd wanted this.

It was also the drinking at night that did it.

Besides, she did not eat much.

At dawn, she awoke and tried to meditate on one of the readings in her father's prayer book. She did not speak out loud, mindful of those who were sleeping off a bad night.

There was a community centre about a kilometre to the north where she went each morning to wash herself. Afterwards, she would buy a cheese sandwich and an apple, eat the sandwich and save the fruit for lunch. She was not hungry; she could not eat without feeling ill.

She never left the tent without her backpack. Close to Bloor Street, the Lower Don area offered access to her bank. She kept both her card and her PIN number in the Velcro-tabbed secret compartment of a zippered jacket pocket, so that once a week, she could go to the bank to make a small withdrawal from the money that was supposed to pay her rent. The first time she ventured out of the ravine, she went to the Central Library to check her email. Her mother had written her. "Just wondering what's going on, Alison. I happen to know that you are not in school. Please send your address." She answered, "I will return to school when I'm ready. I'm eighteen years old now, and I must learn to make decisions for myself. For now, I'd prefer not to give my address. I would like to be alone to think about my life. Please don't worry. I am not in any kind of trouble. I am safe."

Returning to her tent, she fed the squirrels, then greeted Mike, an older, bearded man who wore his grey hair in a ponytail, who wrote poetry on paper napkins and birchbark. Then, she would retreat to her tent to read and meditate. If I survive, I will live as a hermit, she thought.

I want to be good, as I once was.

The world her father had given her was blessed, even if she was not.

Hung in a meat locker, dangling from a hook, was how she felt.

Sometimes, it hurt too much to eat. The alcohol eased the pain of the hook at night.

She cast the weight of its pain aside by reading and feeding the squirrels, by naming the autumn birds.

The Hawk That Had Frightened Her

ALISON SHARED HER PAST WITH NO ONE in Boston, including her falcon. When she fell into the grip of memory, she knew enough not to frighten herself, to entice Daisy to the glove with a treat, to take her walking through the dark veil of time and forgetting. Yet first came remembering, an early morning in the ravine, the day when she got up, bundled in the old padded jacket that kept her warm at night. As she stepped out of the tent, she could hear a fierce beating of wings against the chill dawn air. It was more of a commotion than usual, even for a large bird, but when she looked up, she caught a glimpse of an unmistakable hawk: brown-backed, flame-coloured tail, heavy dark streaking on its underside as it dove down from the sky, an inattentive squirrel in its sights. Its talons sank into the plump, grey creature, the great raptor crushing it with a rhythmic pulverizing motion, squeezing out the last remains of the animal's life. Satisfied that the squirrel was dead, the hawk scooped it up, then settled on a thick branch to skin and eat its meal. I bet I fed that squirrel peanuts, thought Alison.

Then she remembered Princess, the hawk that had frightened her years ago. Dad, she thought, did you send me a red-tailed hawk? A sign that she could redeem herself.

She watched the hawk devour the squirrel, then lick the blood and stringy flesh off her claws. *Don't make like you're squeamish.* Sex with Wendell, the things she did to make him happy, her mouth full of slime. "Enjoy it," he whispered. And she had.

Wild animal.

She imagined it and tasted blood.

At that moment, the hawk flew down from the tree and landed on her arm. Grateful for the padded jacket, Alison felt the lightness of the great bird, then looked into the depth of its eyes, sure that dwelling in the raptor was mystery lit by a spark of awareness; a creature designed for survival and procreation, for some larger end that she could not discern. In spring, the hawk would brood on her eggs, would keep her hatchlings warm.

She wished she could tell her father what she felt. So, she spoke out loud to him, unaware of footsteps approaching her tent. Surprised, Mike looked down at her. "Who ya talking to?"

"My dad."

"Don't see no phone."

"Don't need one. He's always with me."

Mike told her that he understood.

"Where'd you get that hawk?" he asked.

She told him it had stopped by for breakfast.

"Maybe bring you luck, eh?"

"My father sent her. She's a good hawk. She'll protect us."

Mike looked sad. "Hope so," he said.

"Isn't she beautiful?"

"Maybe I'll write a hawk poem," he said, and then he looked hard at Alison. "Take care now," he said, then left.

The hawk lifted her wings, stood tall, then flew away.

Alison noticed bloodstains on her jacket sleeve. The hawk, she felt sure, would be back.

Every night, Alison fed peanuts to the rodents, and every morning, the hawk returned to prey on the creatures that

Alison had fed the night before. One day the earth will feed on all of us, she'd think. She wondered about the afterlife, if the soul outlived its suffering. Or, if it were blessing enough to decompose, to rest in the peace of the earth.

In the morning, the hawk lit on her arm, and with great gentleness, she stroked the feathers on its breast with the back of her hand. *I'm making up for the way I hated Princess.*

At night, she made sure to sleep in her oldest padded jacket, to protect her arm from the great hawk's talons when she came to perch in the early morning.

Alison told Mike and Frieda and anyone who would listen that she was fattening up the rats to feed the hawk. She was aware that if it hadn't been for Mike — and even with his confirmation — the others would have found it hard to believe the story of her feathered visitation, much less her efforts at keeping it fed. They would wonder what junk she was popping as they looked at her with pity.

Her Father's Voice

"YOU SHOULD GO TO MASS, ALISON," her father said in her dream. "That will help you sort things out." His voice was so loud that it woke her up, and she could not get back to sleep. Not knowing what else to do, she noticed the copy of *The Varsity* lying underneath her backpack — the university paper she'd received from the man at the subway entrance, his kind response to the toonie she had given him. She glanced at the newspaper's date — noting that it was still autumn, 2003. In fact, she kept a pocket calendar, and, for the most part, took care to cross off passing dates. It pleased her to find an article about a philosophical symposium of some kind being held at the east end of the campus because it turned out that St. Basil's Church would host a Mass for both the attendants and the student body — not just for Catholics, but for anyone of any faith. Today. On the St. Mike's campus, she thought. It's not that far.

The place will be crawling with priests, she thought.

One of them should say a Mass down here. In the ravine.

She remembered the man who looked like her dad, the one she'd followed, the one she thought was an Anglican priest. *He'll be there for sure. Doesn't matter what religion he is.*

She had an idea. From her backpack, she pulled out a notebook and pen and wrote: "*Dear Father, I would like to thank whoever the priest was who kindly gave me a subway token*

191

and change for coffee. Maybe it was you. Even if it was not, I want to tell you that I live in the Don Valley Ravine. There are many people here who pray and who need your blessing. Would you (or one of your brothers) come here to say Mass for us? We are at the first underpass south of the Bloor Viaduct. We have nothing to give you, only our gratitude. Thank you. Alison."

She asked Mike to keep an eye on her tent, telling him that she was off to Mass, that she planned to find a priest, and that she wanted to invite him here.

"Good luck," said Mike.

"You don't think someone'll come?"

"Why would they?"

She saw what his eyes said. *Nutbar.*

He'd asked her once or twice if she were taking drugs, warning her that there was some bad stuff going around.

No, she wasn't taking drugs; she'd be all right. Alison strapped on her backpack, then made her way out of the ravine, to a bus downtown.

Sunt Lacrimae Rerum

ST. BASIL'S CHURCH WAS ENORMOUS, and, she thought, soot-stained and rather ugly. Yet inside it was brightly lit and filling up with academics and clergy. With relief, she noticed that there were a great many students in pullovers and jeans, young people not much older than herself, their Mass marking the start of the 2003 fall term. She edged her way into the church, aware that she was drawing stares, fearful that her large backpack would bump and jostle her fellow worshippers, wondering if she'd managed to scrub herself clean enough, fearful that she might reek of accumulated garbage and rancid food. Maybe she'd grown used to the unwashed scent of the homeless that made people frown and turn away, but she wasn't one to judge this. She had caught a glimpse of her unkempt, bristled hair as she'd walked past Tim Hortons on her way down Bay Street. Cropped short like a convict's, she thought.

She remembered that her father had replied, "God loves us all. No matter who we are or what we've done."

Alison didn't dare drag her backpack into a pew, fearing it would take up too much space. Instead, she went to the rear of the church, put her pack behind the last pew and used it as a seat.

It was then that she became aware that a man was watching her. He was seated in one of a few extra chairs placed behind the pew across from her. The man was young, dark-haired, wearing a V-necked sweater-vest, crisp shirt, silk tie, and slacks. His clothes were fresh and new, and not casual student attire. All at once she felt shabby, too thin, her getup of worn jeans and sweatshirt unfit for this place. Embarrassed, she could feel his eyes idly toying with her body, and when she looked up, she saw vague disgust in them as if he had imagined holding her at arm's-length and removing her putrid clothes with a pair of surgical forceps. Ashamed of these thoughts, she knelt on the stone floor, bowed her head and prayed to be relieved of them. Then she sat up and joined in the opening prayers of the Mass. Yet she could feel the man's eyes, hard at work at the unpleasant task of undressing her.

Then up ahead, she noticed the man she had followed on the subway some weeks back. He was not wearing a Roman collar, but he was seated with some priests, so she assumed he was an Anglican.

She tried to forget both these men, to stay focused on the Mass, hoping that God had forgiven her for the terrible mistake she had made with Wendell. She prayed to her father for help and guidance. She prayed for her new friends, Mike and Willie and crazy Frieda and the owl who hooted in the night and the red-tailed hawk who came to sit on her arm and the squirrels that scurried through the trees above her tent, and the rats and mice that she fed for the hawks. And she prayed for healing. She went to Communion. Afterwards, she remembered to pray for Edward, the kind man who vanished from her father's life. Feeling in need of help, she prayed for everything and everyone, as if — despite what her father had taught her — prayers could reach God more effectively in church than whispered at night, on her knees, to the stars.

Yet her prayers at night were larger than herself. They also embraced the trees and the sky.

Such a sorrowful place, this world was. She still missed her dad.
"Sunt lacrimae rerum," wrote Virgil.
There are tears at the heart of things.

Seated at the back of the church, Alison was among the first
to leave when Mass was over. She stood near the foot of the
stairs, watching the congregants exit until she saw the man
with a kind and intelligent look, so very much like her father's.
Yet she was distressed to see that he was talking with two
distinguished-looking gentlemen, along with the young man
who had eyed her in the church. She edged over to the priest
whom she'd recognized, so he'd know she was there.

She caught his eye, and he turned away. "I have something
I would like to give you," she said.

He turned to look at her. She saw no sign of recognition in
his face.

"It's a thank you," she said. "And a request."

He looked puzzled.

"You gave me a token last week. And a toonie." His look of
sudden recognition faded into one of suspicion, and she saw
it in his eyes. *What does she want now?*

"Prayers," she said. "That's all."

She handed him the note. She was about to leave when the
young man took out his digital camera, aimed it in her direction
and startled her by taking her picture. Why did he do that? she
wondered as the men moved away from her. The young man
turned and spoke to the man she thought of as a priest, and
the two of them eyed her, as if she were a road sign pointing
in the wrong direction. The priest whispered something in the
young man's ear as she walked away.

"Well, that took guts." It was that irritating man, following her
down the path. Alison looked at him, perplexed. "That priest

is world-renowned. He's a guest of the college president and my dad, and they were on their way to lunch at Sassafraz."

"So I should care?" She'd never heard of Sassafraz.

"You could always chase them down." *Maybe shake them down, while you're at it,* his look said.

"I don't need to," she said.

"Okay, so he might invite you. Corporal work of mercy."

I guess I must look pretty bad, she thought. Then she recovered her composure. "I have lunch in my pack," she said as she left.

Alison strode north up Bay Street, then east on Bloor to the big library, where she parked herself in the lobby and dug into her backpack for her peanut butter sandwich. Having gone to Mass, she had felt calmed by the ritual, by the words of blessing. Then, this priest turned his back on her and this snotty showoff came along and smacked her down. *I'm not hungry anyway.* Her stomach hurt, and she started to cry.

There's no point crying, she thought. *You're here to sort things out.*

"I'm here to help you," said her dad. "I know it's hard."

She dried her eyes.

Splinter

IF SHE SEES A LEAF FALL, she prays in thanksgiving for its life. If she sees a migrating thrush, she prays for its safety. Whenever she can, she prays for the hawk and the owl and the mice they eat, and so she feels that the least she can do is to pray for this unkind man, whoever he was, so that he might learn compassion.

Maybe God was out of the office, but even so, it calms her to offer prayers, a kid thrown out of the house for screwing her mother's boyfriend. No, more than that. She's a pilgrim, looking for a homeward path, looking to draw the splinter of remorse out from underneath her skin. This is a slow and painful task, but it helps her turn her mind to others, and so in pain and adversity she prays.

At night, after she drinks cheap wine with her companions in the ravine, she prays for herself because she fears she's gotten a taste for it. She's afraid she will lose the path through the dark.

The Same Man

THE FOLLOWING MORNING, as the hawk fled and the autumn light spilled honey on the grass, she went to wash at the community centre. Someone spat out, "Fucking street kids," as she emerged from the lavatory. "Turning this place into a shit-hole." But she thought to herself that this was an ignorant person, and she had grown used to offering prayers, so she'd add this man to the list.

Yet on this particular morning, while she prayed for someone who'd insulted her, she recalled the cheap wine from the night before, and started to fear its power over her. Then, as she headed back to her tent along the deserted bike path, she saw him.

The same man who insulted her.

The same man outside the church.

He carried himself with the sculpted grace of statuary. "Well-bred," her mom once said of her own boss. "Like a horse." The memory of her sharp words slapped the air with a warning. Smart, clean clothes, dark hair, strange, unhappy eyes — grey, like rancid butter.

"I followed you," he said. "I wanted to apologize. "

She looked at him, a man not much older than herself.

"I want you to understand that I'm not out to harm you," he said. He never took his eyes off her, as if he needed her reply to give him peace.

As she wondered how to answer, she recognized his face. "I met you at church," she said.

"Yes, I recall. I'm a student. My name's Gavin." He paused. "Do you have email?"

"Yes. I'm Alison."

"I took a picture of you, Alison. It's very nice." He pulled out his camera and showed her the image on the screen. He'd caught an expression of bewildered innocence. She looked much younger than eighteen. He took her email address and promised to send her the photo. She told him she'd print it out on her next library visit.

"Do you live near here?" she asked.

"First you must tell me why you're living like this." He spoke with great intensity that also felt like profound concern, as if he knew her and wanted to help her.

She felt stirred by his words, yet wary. It was personal, she explained. She couldn't live at home anymore. She needed time to think and reflect, to read and pray. Like going on a retreat.

He paused, then spoke. "You're not like those rummies on the other side of the underpass," he said. "You don't belong there."

"For now, I do," she said. She felt a kind of fearless relief, strength in admitting the truths of her humble life, so she went ahead and told him that the folks he called rummies were suffering souls, that he mustn't malign her troubled friends, that they were in need of kindness. She told him about their visitor, a red-tailed hawk that perched on her sleeve, a watchful, graceful presence, sent to her through the grace of her father's spirit.

She could see that he pitied her, that he thought she was out of her mind, that his tangled heart loved and hated everything she'd said.

"You have no one to look after you," he whispered. "It isn't safe to live like this."

"My father's looking out for me."

"I hope so."

He carried a great stillness, she thought, his breathing shallow, as if he were afraid yet full of longing.

Book Club

GAVIN MOORE WAS STUDYING ENGLISH at the University of Toronto in the fall 2003 semester. "I have only afternoon classes," he said, a formal announcement that seemed odd to her, as if he were reporting on the actions of some other *he*. The young man lived not far from here, on Rosedale Valley Road. He came walking in the ravine every morning.

"Why don't you come home with me?" he said. "You could have a shower, do some laundry."

"I don't know you."

He looked abashed, almost confused. "What a thing for me to ask," he said, as if he were talking to some renegade self, a cheeky character he hadn't known was there.

As if he were reading from the wrong page of a script, she thought.

"I'm all right as I am," she said. "Really."

"But for how long?"

"Right now, this is my life. I love nature. I can't bear to be indoors." Then she told him that her father used to say we were here on earth to find God, to dwell in some deep and abiding mystery. She wanted the life of a pilgrim. Gavin listened.

"You're a good person," he said, his voice gentle. "Courteous and thoughtful. Not worldly, like the rest of us." He paused. "Do you like to read?"

Yes, she told him, and he said he had loads of good books:

novels, poetry, literary works; that he'd like to make up for his lack of kindness, for the harshness of his judgment by lending her something nourishing while she was living in the ravine. Out of his backpack he pulled a copy of Tolstoy's *The Death of Ivan Ilyitch*, and he told her to enjoy it, to come back to this spot any day at this time, since he didn't have morning classes.

She read it that afternoon, and when she found her way down the light-strewn trail the following morning, Gavin was there, leaning against a tree, arms folded, as if he were expecting her. When she returned Tolstoy's slender work to him, he said, "Book club's in session," and then he dug inside his pouch. "Got some good weed, want some?"

"No, thank you," she said, but he'd rolled it and lit it, and it seemed rude to decline, so she took a drag. She didn't like it.

"I don't want to live in a fog," she said. "Not when I need to find my way."

"I understand." He finished the toke, and they talked about Tolstoy's dying character who entered into a silent mystery at the moment of his death.

"This book was a gift," she said to him. "Thank you."

"Dear Alison, I have a surprise for you."

"Another book?"

He leaned over to her, about to kiss her on the mouth, but she pulled away. "I just want to be friends," she said.

"But you're beautiful." He paused. "Alison, I apologize. I should have asked first. Are you gay?"

"No."

"Have you ever…"

"Think of me as a nun."

"A novice? They can always back out…"

"Final vows."

"Whatever." Gavin shrugged, dug into his pack, pulled out a copy of Emily Dickinson's poems and handed them to her.

"Shut away in her castle," he said. "The cloistered life intrigues me."

"I love her poetry."

"My little bird in a cage," he said. He smiled, but not with his eyes.

I Fear for You

SHE HAD ONLY MET HIM YESTERDAY, and already he'd made a pass at her. It sure isn't because of the way I'm dressed, she thought. Her hair looked like it was cut by a chainsaw. Her jeans were ripped, her jacket sleeve's been shredded by a hawk, and there were bloodstains all over it from the dead rat the raptor ate. She was as skinny as a hydro pole, and her clothes were falling off.

Maybe that was it, she thought. *Baggy clothes. Easy to cop a feel that way.*

Yet at the same time, Gavin struck her as harmless, an awkward guy with his nose in a book, clueless about girls and their feelings. She was struck by his strange combination of brains and clumsiness, his stumbling into friendship through poetry and prose, his blundering confusion and eagerness to make amends. There was nothing smooth about him. I've got a few rough edges myself, she thought. Remembering their encounter at the church, she had asked him how he knew such important people.

"How do you mean?" he said.

"That priest I spoke to. You knew where he was eating lunch."

"This is sort of embarrassing," he said. "I'll sound like a show-off."

"No, tell me."

"My dad knows the president of the college," he continued.

"Dad made a donation, so he was invited to the lunch."

Alison didn't know what to say.

"See, I told you. You think I'm a show-off," he said.

"No," she replied. "I just never expected to run into..."

"...a rich guy hanging out in the Don Valley Ravine. Go on, say it."

"No. You don't understand. I didn't expect to meet anyone here. I told you, I'm sort of a hermit."

"You're a very different kind of girl." He looked hard at her, and then he took her hands in his and said, "I fear for you."

No one had ever feared for her.

He was so intense. A little strange. Like her.

"My dear hawk friend, you see how weak I am," she told the creature when it came to perch on her arm the following morning. "Last night, I dreamt about Gavin. He held me, rocked me back and forth. He said he wanted to protect me." The hawk eyed her with supreme indifference. She was preening, removing a torn bit of flesh from her talons.

But I've made things clear to Gavin, she thought. *Besides, it was just a dream.*

Marguerite

A WOMAN THE OTHERS CALLED MAGGIE came by that afternoon. Alison didn't care for that name, wondering what her real name was. She had heard Mike and Frieda mention her, and she assumed she must be a social worker. "She'll be coming for you soon, my sweetheart," said Frieda. "They check out the kids here; they like to take them away."

Let her try, thought Alison. Yet she had no plan, no idea of what she might do if the authorities (whoever they might be) should come to remove her from the ravine. She was an adult, free to decide for herself where she wanted to live.

She sat outside her tent, reading Emily Dickinson. "*Hope is the thing with feathers—/ That perches in the soul....*" Then she looked up, felt footsteps crunching the autumn leaves, caught a glimpse of a pair of beige running shoes, the cheap, old-lady kind you might pick up at Honest Ed's, then faded jeans and a dull beige nylon jacket. The woman crouched down beside Alison — pale face, long white hair drawn back in a clasp. She looked as if she belonged in the encampment, as if a large eraser had smudged her colours from the page of life. She was lugging a small thermos bin.

"My name's Maggie," she said.

"Is that your real name?"

"It's Marguerite. But they like to call me Maggie."

Alison eyed the woman. "Are you French?"

The woman said yes, that she'd grown up near Sudbury in Northern Ontario.

"My mother taught me French," said Alison.

"And where is your mother?"

"In Montreal with her boyfriend."

She felt Maggie's gaze, her dark eyes betraying a deep sadness. She had an honest look that softened the planes and angles of her face.

"But she left you behind."

"There was trouble at home. It's partly my fault. I have to think about things." She watched Maggie, her eyes taking in the tent, its open flap, the crucifix suspended from a metal strut, the sack of peanuts, her backpack and books. The woman explained that she was here to help, to let her know where she might find medical assistance or relief from drugs or counselling or a hot meal; that she came by every week to visit.

"I want to stay here," said Alison. "As much as I can."

"You like these woods, is that it?"

"My father loved the woods. He told me to come here."

"And where is he?"

"He passed away." She told her about the owl sent by her father who came by night to watch over her, the protective hawk her father had loved who flew to her side every morning, her task of feeding the squirrels and mice, how comforting these creatures were. Maggie took her hand in hers. "And what does your father say to you now?"

"He tells me to be patient, to see God in everything."

"Alison, you're very brave," she said. *And much too thin.* Alison could read her face.

"Don't make me leave."

"I won't do that. But I'd like to give you something to eat." She dug into her bin, opened a thermos, and poured some hot chicken broth into a cup. Alison reached out to take it, but her hands were shaking. Maggie put the cup down, found a blanket in Alison's tent and wrapped it around her shoulders.

Afraid of looking weak, Alison tried to stop herself from shivering. Maggie fed her, spooning the broth into her mouth.

Bird in a Cage

MAGGIE CAME TO VISIT EVERY WEEK, and she brought Alison some warm clothes, a winter overcoat and boots, hot soup and sandwiches. She was a nun, a modern one, who lived with some other nuns in a house downtown.

"Maybe you taught at my school," said Alison. As it turned out, she learned that Maggie used to go to church in her parish; a tall, spare woman who would stand at the altar reading the scriptures during Mass.

"My dad used to say he liked the way you read," she said. "Like you meant it." Maggie told her that she was a student then, studying to be a social worker.

Alison lapsed into silence. She did not want to say anything that might provide the woman with a tool, however gentle, to unravel the ugly chrysalis from which she would one day emerge. Hanging from a branch, bound in frail skin, she slipped inside an invisible glass jar, a tight seal on the lid. Her safe place, whenever Maggie came.

"Do you know we're into November?" the woman asked her. "It's going to snow soon. You have to keep warm."

Alison shook her head, no. She felt puzzled, that she had lost track of time, but she'd lost the little notebook-calendar where she used to mark off the dates. Yet she'd arrived here in September; she knew this because her mother had moved on Labour Day, but she had thought that only a month had passed. "I don't know what day it is," she answered.

"Alison, how are you feeling?" the woman asked, and she replied, "I'm fine," but Maggie persisted. "No, I mean about your life."

And so Alison replied, "When I came here, I thought it would be like a retreat. I enjoy the outdoors, camping with just a few things. I want a simple life. I pray to God and feed the squirrels. I'm trying to get down to what's important, so I read a lot." She paused. "Sometimes, I drink."

"You're still young," said Maggie. "Your whole life's ahead."

"I don't know how long I have," she replied.

"Do you need help, dear?" Maggie took her hand and held it between hers while Alison thought of what her life had become, how she drank more than she used to, and how when she saw Gavin a week ago, he said, "Got some great weed, sure you don't want to try?" and she had changed her mind, smoked up because she felt cold and lonely and the weed cheered her, and made her look at him with the hard, bright eyes of animal wanting. "My sweet little bird in a cage," he had whispered, and she had longed for him then.

There was no help for that. She knew better than to sleep with Gavin, but even so, these were not feelings that a nun would understand, even a modern one. Yet she could sense Maggie's eyes on her. *Do you need help, dear?* as if she were waiting for an answer.

Protection

HER GREATEST SOLACE WAS READING. She bought weed from Gavin and smoked it in the tent, borrowed and read his books: Joyce, Woolf, Faulkner, O'Connor, Dickinson. They would meet in the morning and talk about them, and one day, Gavin drew close and stroked her hair and told her that he was here to protect her, that she must not be afraid of him. She let herself go limp in his arms. He did not rock her back and forth as he had in her dream but held her instead like a package in the mail, delivered into his hands at last.

Snow Globe

ALISON DECIDED TO STOP DRINKING. She told the others in the encampment that she was not sleeping well. No longer putting money in the kitty for cheap booze, she saved the cash for Gavin's quality weed. By now, she had realized that the well-read student did a lucrative business in drugs on the side, and the fact that she was no more than a client brought relief. Yet his sales tactics struck her as odd, luring her with books and conversation as a way of enticing her to try his product. She feared he might try to lure her with heroin, and she prayed to God that she would not be weak. By night, she asked the owl for protection.

One morning, she awoke to greet the red-tailed hawk in a world transformed by frost and falling snow. It was December. Maggie had given her a calendar so she could enter time, so that she could draw a line through each passing day, but Alison did not want the splendour of today to be hidden by the indifferent stroke of a pen. She had woken up inside a snow globe, suspended in a timeless moment, a glittering world transformed, an image of the soul's transformation that she longed for.

Yet today was a Monday. *Bank day; email Mom day.* She spent time with the hawk, fed some peanuts to the squirrels, then took her pack and headed through the ravine to the community centre for her morning wash. Along the trail, she strode through drifts, in awe of the white silence, the dust and sparkle of snow on a squirrel's tail, the red flash of a cardinal on a bough. Adrift as she knew herself to be, she felt at peace.

When she reached the washroom door, she found it locked.

"First of December, that's when they lock it for the winter." Gavin stepped out from behind the trees. "You didn't know that?" he asked.

"Why would they lock it?"

"They just do. No one comes here in winter."

"I'll have to find another place."

"Uh-uh. City-wide, they're all closed," he said. He paused, as if he were trying to come up with a solution. "Alison, come to my place," he said at last. "Get yourself a shower. Do some laundry if you have to."

She didn't say anything. She did not think to ask why he had come at this early hour.

"It isn't far. Come on."

She followed him. Later, she would say that it had something to do with silence, with the peculiar spell of that first snowfall. Otherwise, she might not have followed along.

Gavin lived in an apartment building on Rosedale Valley Road, on the building's eighth and topmost floor. When they stepped out of the elevator and into his apartment, she stood in the foyer, unable to move. The sight of it left her in shock. She had forgotten that such beauty and cleanliness might still exist in the world, such enormous windows gathering up an intensity of sunlight as if they were magnifying glasses, as if she were paper that might be set afire if she stood before them.

"Don't look so shocked," said Gavin. "It's called a *home*."

She felt as if she had left the world. Beautiful and light, floating above everything. His parents are well off, she thought. Gleaming, honey-coloured parquet floors, a spacious living-room area with simple quality furnishings and shelves of books. All of it spotless, pristine. Apart from one or two framed posters, the walls were bare.

"You're thinking, 'What's a student doing in these digs?'" he said.

"Yeah, I guess I was."

"See? I know you well enough to read your mind. My parents want me to study hard, that's why."

"Where do they live?"

"A few blocks away. They're in Florida now."

"Just in time for the snow," she said. She didn't know what else to say.

"I'll be joining them for Christmas." He showed her the bathroom.

"It's ... very beautiful," she said.

"Been awhile, huh, Allie?"

"I guess." She felt very small. He laughed as she gazed at its recessed lighting, marble appointments, thick towels, an array of bathing supplies, brushes, cosmetics, grooming implements. He handed her a warm flannel bathrobe. It looked brand new.

"Enjoy," he said. "Dump your clothes outside the door. I'll throw them in the wash."

"They won't be done by the time I'm finished."

"Bet they will. You've got lots to keep you busy in that shower. I'll make us tea, and by then, they'll be done."

Gavin was right. She scrubbed and showered, washed and dried her hair, enjoying the luxury of a thorough cleaning, of doing all of her grooming tasks and taking her time with them. It puzzled her that his bathroom was so well equipped. Maybe he has a girlfriend, she thought. It took her an hour. She bundled up in the thick robe and made her way into the kitchen.

"Guess I was pretty grubby," she said. "Sorry I took so long."

"Not at all." He had just poured tea, he told her, and they

sat at the dining-room table. She noticed a plate of oatmeal cookies.

"Friend of mine made those," he said. "Hungry?"

"Not very, thank you."

"Let's split one." He broke a cookie, then poured her a large and fragrant cup of tea. "Chinese herbal mix," he said. "My parents brought it back from Shanghai. Nice with a cookie dunked in it."

She tried the cookie but preferred the tea. It was easy to drink — aromatic and not too hot. Gavin was talking to her, his voice a gentle and soporific whisper. She inhaled the fragrant tea and drank. "Want more?" asked Gavin from the other side of the room.

"Yes, please," she said.

Outside, the snow swirled, and the sun began to spin, a loose and ghastly eyeball in a cloudy socket, and the great hawk sank its talons into the world and drew blood, then lifted its wings and flew away forever, and the beautiful pristine room began its slow tilt sideways and she could feel herself sliding downward, wondering where Gavin was and if he would pick her up, and he did. He lifted her in his arms before she fell unconscious, but before she did, she could feel her slight limbs as weighty as the trunks of trees, an animal's teeth piercing her breasts; his hands, his hard soul shoved into her body while her insides shuddered and memory died.

Brush Cut

SHE SLEPT AND WOKE UP to the fading light of afternoon. Gavin walked into the bedroom. "Let's get you up," he said.

She still felt woozy, could not remember anything. He helped her to stand, put on her robe, brought her into the bathroom. "Didn't know you enjoyed that stuff," he said.

She didn't know what he was talking about.

"You wore me out." He sat her on the toilet, then pulled out a set of hair clippers and a razor. "Been dying to give you a haircut since the day I met you," he said.

Alison was too tired to object. He trimmed her spiky hair close to the skull. From what she could see in the mirror, it was at least tidy.

"I get off on girls with brush cuts," he said.

"It looks very nice."

"You like it?"

"Yes."

"My little bird in a cage." He ran his hands over her head, her face, her neck. He kissed her neck and breathed into her ear. "Feel good?"

"Yes," she said, because she was afraid to say no.

He ran his hands over her breasts. "Now we'll do it awake."

"I want to go home."

"You don't have a home."

Gavin picked her up and flung her over his shoulder like a

sack of refuse. He walked into the bedroom, threw her on the bed, pinned her down.

Job Offer

NIGHT HAD FALLEN. She got up from the bed, a bitter taste in her mouth. She was afraid she might vomit. "I would like to use the washroom."

He smiled at her, but not with his eyes. "Yes, of course, Alison. You need a break."

His tone of voice was formal, detached, as if she were his student, as if she had performed well.

As she walked to the bathroom, she noticed her laundry, washed, dried, and folded into neat piles on the dining-room table, all of it done while she slept off the drug. This fastidious man, obsessive and tidy about his person and hers, was so revolted by her homeless state that he'd done this to her. He'd planned it, preyed on her for months, and she fell into the trap. She was afraid she would never leave this place alive.

"You'll need your clothes," he said to her.

"Thank you for taking care of them."

"My pleasure."

Alison dressed quickly.

"You don't want to stay? We could have supper."

"I'm exhausted."

"I'll walk you back," he said.

"No need." It was eight o'clock, early enough for a safe walk.

He looked hesitant. "A girl like you needs someone to protect her. There are worse men out on the street than me."

"I don't understand."

"You won't have money forever. I can get you work."

She looked at him, perplexed.

"I can bring you clients. We can split the take."

Alison thought she might faint. "I don't need the money," she said.

"I'll give you my card," he said. "In case you change your mind."

She took his card and put it in her pocket.

"You're not angry with me, angel?"

How she felt was beyond anger. Yet if she said she was, he would tell her she had provoked him. She said nothing.

"Never mind, I'll know where to find you. In the ravine, beyond the underpass. Cute little blue pup tent, right? Peanut shells all over." He grabbed her by the shoulders and kissed her hard on the mouth, a searing and painful kiss. She felt branded by the heat of it, her flesh cauterized so that nothing good would grow there, his mark burned into her skin.

Her Burden

SHE FOUND HER WAY BACK through the snow to the ravine, and as soon as she began her downward meander to the encampment near the underpass, she leaned against a tree and threw up. Her body felt raw, eviscerated, as if her guts had been scraped out — a dead chicken hung from a hook. *That's all I am, all I'll ever be. A hollow for someone's hand to dig in and play with. Why did I let this happen, why?* "Because he drugged you," a voice answered. *No, but why did I even go to his house?* She was remembering Maggie, who'd given her a card that listed places to get a shower and a hot meal. *It's your own damn fault. You didn't think.* She could feel his hands, his mouth, as she had with Wendell, as if what the drug had erased from memory would be reclaimed by the senses, by her body waiting in ambush to destroy her.

She stopped by a snowbank to wash her face, and she felt something damp between her legs. Her period wasn't due. She would stuff some pads in there and hope the bleeding stopped. Now, she remembered: "Tell me you like this," he'd whispered, and she'd said, "I like it," because he had his hands on her neck, and then he turned her over. She still had some weed and that would kill the pain.

It was cold in the tent. Maybe this will be my last night on earth, but at least my clothes are clean, she thought. She looked up at the crucifix, at the man condemned, at the suffering that was also hers. *Except that I was just plain stupid.* She had never believed that Jesus Christ had died for people's sins. She thought it was much simpler, that he died because people hated him. *Sunt lacrimae rerum.* She took the crucifix down and stuffed it in her backpack, so she might carry her own burden and ponder that innocent man, as her father had taught her to do.

Only she could not live with what she had endured.

There was a subway nearby. There was a river. Bundled up in all her clothes, she smoked the last of her weed.

The owl did not call that night.

In the morning, the hawk did not return.

Password

ALISON KNEW THAT SHE COULD not remain here, that she would have to leave the ravine, that Gavin would hunt her down. So would Maggie, who she hoped never to meet again. Having done this to herself, she could not bear to face a woman who had tried to help her. When Mike waved her down, she told him she was headed for the bank and the library, and so she left the tent behind, strapped on her backpack, and made her way to Yonge and Bloor, where there were dozens of ATMs at her branch and no lineups, no one to stare or turn away from an unkempt kid with butch hair and a tattered, oversized pack.

In the lobby of the building, she unzipped her pocket and felt for her bank card in its hidden pocket with the Velcro strip. She couldn't find it, retrieving it instead from a second pocket that was just as secure. *That's weird. I'm sure I didn't put it there.* She went to the ATM, inserted the card, punched in the password.

"VOID," said the message. "ACCOUNT CLOSED."

The account had no money in it.

She had been careful to keep track. It was money her mother had given her.

Gavin — who else? But how did he get my PIN?

She'd written it down on a small card concealed in that same secret compartment in the breast pocket of her jacket. He must have ransacked her belongings while she slept, emptied out

222

her bank account over the phone, leaving her broke, desperate and open to his offer of steady work in bed. He was probably sitting by the phone right now, waiting for her to call.

He planned this. From the time we met at the church. From the first damned book he loaned me. And I fell for it.

In shock, Alison crossed the street to the library and made her way to the public computers. She logged on, took a deep breath and clicked on an email from her mother. "Dear Alison," the woman wrote, "I hope all is well with you. I realize that you have your parents' strong sense of adventure, a strong need to be on your own. I won't interfere, except to tell you that all is forgiven. I want you to know that."

Alison didn't know what to do. Her mistake, losing the money, writing down her password. *Forgiven.* If her mom knew how stupid she'd been, she would never forgive her.

"Dear Mom," she wrote. "We had our first winter snow. I'm reading a lot and realizing that life is not easy. I need a chance to sort things out. Thank you for forgiving me."

She read the email over, then remembered that her mother no longer wanted to be addressed by a title. She deleted, *"Mom."*

"Dear Jeannette," she wrote.

Moments later, her mother replied. "You are so much like your father. You have his voice."

It Was Time

ONLY SHE NO LONGER HEARD his voice, no longer had him to guide her. Unwell, as if she were hanging from a meat hook buried in her insides.

She should go to the doctor. Only she didn't want to get well. She wanted to disappear like a fallen leaf, a squirrel crushed under the wheels of a car. A street-corner derelict buried under blankets, invisible, safer than in the ravine, where Gavin would find her, kidnap her, do worse. On Yonge Street, she saw a garbage bin. She pulled from her backpack pouch the cards that Maggie had given her — for clinics, a hot meal, a shower, the woman's own address and phone — and she pitched them all in the trash.

She refused to beg, would not become a lump of blankets by the side of the road, a paper cup in her hand. She would only draw hatred and contempt, and she had more than enough of that for herself. Worse, Gavin might go on the prowl and spot her.

"I only give to buskers in the subway," she said to a friend once. "My mom says beggars on the street'll just drink it away."

The shadows of the late day were tumbling down on her. Snow was falling like flour through a sieve of cloud, and she was too exhausted and in too much pain to go on, so she found herself a laneway off Yonge Street, stumbled and fell behind the rough backsides of restaurants, pubs, sex shops, garbage bins, and the anemic blur of red, blue, green, and yellow Christmas lights. Heat by the rear walls, good for awhile. She burrowed down, hoping never to open her eyes again.

Someone

YET SHE DID. MORNING FOUND HER ALIVE, huddled under
blankets near a heating grate, drifting between sleep and wake-
fulness, and she remembered the hawk that used to watch over
her, but she had been afraid of hawks as a child so her father
sent it away, and now all she sees is the rumble of the street
beyond the laneway, glad there was no one here to step over
her, to take a kick at a shameful hand reaching out to beg for
change. The snow was falling again, and that was when she
felt certain that Gavin must be kneeling beside her. How could
she have missed him sneaking up on her, crouched down and
purring in her ear, tongue licking her body like a rabid cat.
"You wanted me. You were so hot," so it was all her fault, only
she stopped feeling cold hours, days ago. He is the only heat
her body remembers, and she is going to die as he bangs her
like a jackhammer. She can't feel her limbs, just the pain, and
then she hears the sound of a small piece of crockery pushed
in her direction and a *clank-clank*. She opens her eyes. Someone from the restaurant has put a mug beside her, has thrown
in some change. She is now a beggar, in with the back-alley
druggies and hookers, the sick and demented. Someone drops
change in the cup. For sure it's Gavin; he wants to fuck her
for a toonie. She can't stop him, closes her eyes, then opens
them to see in horror the enormous face of someone kneeling
beside her, a woman's face made up of planes and angles and

great, sorrowful eyes, wide and disturbed as a turbulent sky, white-haired, slender, and she feels a hand on her shoulder, doesn't want to feel anything at all.

"Alison," whispers a familiar voice.

She blacks out.

Memory and Warning

FROM HER PERCH, THE FALCON WATCHED, unable to understand the soft cries from her keeper, seated outside the cage, face hidden. At last, the woman sat up, put on her glove, and opened the wire door. She didn't murmur those happy sounds that shaped the air into warmth and the promise of food. Instead, she held out her gloved hand and said nothing. Daisy flew to it, stood tall and stretched her wings. They brushed against warm, wet skin.

Morning, and Alison was grateful for the falcon's presence. When she'd composed herself, she took Daisy out for a walk. A consolation, as memory flowed out of her body and into the patient earth.

In early 2004, she'd lived in a hospital's shadows, its silence, the cool feel of Maggie's hand resting on her forehead, dark sleep and muted voices, and her own: "Why did you look for me? You should have let me die." And the woman's answer, "You're going to get well, you still have so much life to live," because she had gone to the encampment, had learned that the girl had left and had not returned. That was how Maggie found her in the laneway, knowing the derelict places where the young went to die.

There was a therapist, a doctor, a slow breaking of silence. "I won't go to a shelter," said Alison. "I'm afraid to be inside, I'd rather live in the ravine," but in time she listened to Maggie, who chose to blame her illness on camping out in the cold. She offered Alison a spare room in her house on Isabella Street, where day by day, she would clothe her in the garb of civility, with a quiet insistence on her good mind, her need to complete high school, to study and find friends. The law, she added, required her as a social worker to track down her mother. "I guess you'll have to tell her what I did," said Alison.

"In so many words," said Maggie. "Yes."

It was late winter when Alison moved into her new quarters. Because she would not return to school until next fall, she spent time studying with a tutor and reviewing her schoolwork, offering to help around the house in lieu of paying rent. They had given her a small room, a quiet space where she could read and study.

She did not wander far from home. Everything felt tentative, as hesitant as a spring day in Toronto. With the milder weather, she and Maggie would walk west to Queen's Park, its trees in bud and jittery with songbirds. At first, she was afraid to walk alone. She felt terrified, frail as a blade of grass, naked under a terrible sky, the still opacity of God.

The park was close to the university, and she feared running into Gavin Moore. She had been too afraid to press charges, so he had not been caught. "It will happen," said her therapist. "He'll try again, with someone else."

She kept the photo he'd taken of her in front of St. Basil's Church, folded and tucked away in her father's prayer book, an object of memory and warning, like some ancient image of hell that spoke of dire punishment for those who failed to change their ways. I dove into hell when I told him I liked what he was doing to me, but that was because his hands were around my neck, she thought. *And that happened because I came to see him every day, and I let him think he could get away with it.* Remembering the horror, she thought of the ancient image of the snake devouring its tail, sure she could not point to the beginning of her nightmare or its end, still uncertain of who was at fault, who began it.

"We nest in God," said her father. "Tender Bird brooding on the world, save us." The words and the memory of his voice made her cry.

She was ashamed to tell Maggie what happened with Gavin. Instead, she told her that she was sorry for the trouble she'd caused, that she found it hard to forgive herself, that the songbirds gave her hope.

Shame

FOR THE MOST PART, ALISON KEPT TO HERSELF. She eyed the other three sisters in the house, struck by their blandness of manner as they approached her, their sound like the quiet footfalls of nurses in hospital, of people whose normal voices fell on her ears like whispers. Although she had never spoken to any of them about Gavin, she began to realize that they must have known what had happened to her, that Maggie would have heard from the hospital. They were social workers and teachers, exposed to the sorrows of the world, yet Alison sensed that she troubled all of them, that her presence bore witness to a malign power that disturbed their home's tranquillity, that mocked the calmness of daily work and hope.

This saddened her, yet she felt it might be a justified response. Still recovering from the feral lure of the ravine, she believed that she'd done some irreparable damage to herself that nothing could mend. Remorse went beyond the word itself. It was an acid burn, a corrosion of her spirit.

Maggie encouraged her to keep a journal, and at night, she wrote. Thinking of her dad's reflections, she wondered if the hurts inflicted on her body had injured God's as well.

"You didn't cause what happened," said her therapist. "Gavin is a criminal. He had no right to do that."

Yet she couldn't describe the shame that still encased her. She only felt free of it when she watched the birds.

School Days

ALISON'S MOTHER WROTE TO MAGGIE, apologizing for the inconvenience of her daughter's misbehaviour, saying that she was prepared to pay for her enrolment in a first-rate Catholic school. There was one nearby on Wellesley Street — one with a dress code and good discipline — and that she planned to visit as soon as her schedule permitted her to do so. Maggie showed Alison the email. "I can get you into that school," she said.

"Only I feel bad, taking money from my mother."

"It's for the uniform. You have to have one."

Then Alison told her about her bank account, the money her mother had given her to rent a room, how she chose to spend some of it on everyday expenses (including weed) and that the rest was stolen. She fibbed that someone had swiped her PIN number from the pocket of a coat she'd left in her tent.

"You'll feel better if you tell your mom," said Maggie, her voice weary. "Just that someone stole your bank card. That's plenty."

Jeannette

"I WON'T ASK THE CIRCUMSTANCES," wrote her mother, once Alison explained what happened. "I'm glad someone can keep an eye on you. This is your last chance. Is that fair?"

"Yes," Alison wrote. "It's fair. I understand."

"I wrote to Jeannette," she told Maggie.

"Who's Jeannette?"

"My mom."

She registered a pained look on Maggie's face.

"She wants me to use her real name. Not a label."

She showed her what her mom had written and how she'd responded.

"I don't feel any better. I feel worse."

Maggie sighed. "Pray," she said, "that when school starts, you'll forget this ever happened."

Earworm

NONE OF THIS ERASED THE FACT that Alison felt unforgiven. As she recovered, she decided to join the sisters for daily Mass at the church on Sherbourne Street, glad for an hour of quiet ritual and intelligent reflection from a priest who seemed human and friendly enough. The church was an enormous, somewhat kitschy place, one that swallowed and digested its slight congregation in a cavernous maw of silence. No matter; silence was good. She received the Eucharist, but did not take wine. It was hard for her to feel that she belonged here.

One Sunday, she took home a bulletin from the church. When she opened it, her eye caught one word, outlined in a square box:

Reconciliation

It used to be called, "Confession."

I can't, she thought.

It was different now, she knew that. No need to step into a dark closet with a sliding panel and a disembodied voice doling out pious scoldings and three Hail-Marys as penance. If you wanted, you could sit in a room, in a comfortable chair, face to face, like therapy. She heard they even kept Kleenex boxes there.

To do that, you had to make an appointment.

No. That's crazy.

Why the hell would I do it?

Because you feel you did something wrong, not just something stupid. Not just one thing, either.

She couldn't get it out of her mind. *Reconciliation.* The word crawled into her head like those earworms that kept a dumb song spiralling deeper and deeper into her poor, tired brain. What was left of it.

It would drive her nuts until she did something. She could at least check. She could walk out if she didn't like it.

It Had Been A While

SHE MADE THE APPOINTMENT, went to the church, and tapped on the door of the office used as a Reconciliation Room.

The priest let her in. His name was Father Bob, the one who said daily Mass, a young guy with a serious gaze, with moody grey winter in his eyes. Let it snow, she thought, remembering the ravine. *Let it bury me.*

What the fuck am I doing here?

He welcomed her, told her he knew her face from Mass with the sisters.

Alison felt in her pocket for a piece of paper. Before coming, you were supposed to examine your conscience and tick off your sins against each of the ten commandments. She'd taken her time with this. She'd thought of listing her mortal sins in bullet form. Section One, subsection A and so on.

Only she got nervous and forgot the opening prayer she was supposed to say. Instead, she blurted out that she was sorry, that it had been a while since she'd received this sacrament. A few years, maybe.

"I was living in the ravine," she said.

"Have you no home?" the priest asked. His voice was quiet. Intense, as if his whole body were an organ of hearing.

"I had to leave home because I messed up," she began. "I slept with my mother's boyfriend."

Silence.

"I know I shouldn't have. He made it easy, and I did it." She glanced at the sheet of paper. "I don't have the exact number of times."

"How old was this man?"

Alison paused. "My mom's age, I would guess."

"He took advantage of you. Do you realize that?"

"I went along with it."

"You were only ... how old?"

"Seventeen, the first time."

"I know you're sorry and that you shouldn't have done it. But you have been made to carry all the blame."

Alison was not expecting this.

"Mom threw me out of the house," she said. "After she got me the abortion."

Absolute silence. As if some dreaded explosion had ripped their eardrums open. She was afraid that when she spoke again, she would not be able to hear her own words. When she did speak, the sounds seem to come from a distance, as if she were watching a movie.

"I never questioned it," said Alison. " "I felt ashamed for cheating on her."

"How did it make you feel, Alison?"

"The abortion? Not great." She took a deep breath. "Except that I would have killed myself without it."

He was still listening, this priest.

No turning back, she thought. Lowering her eyes, she told him about her life in the ravine, about what had happened with the young man on the bicycle path.

She was afraid to look up, afraid of the chill cold that would fall on her from those wintry eyes. At last, she raised her head and looked into a face so full of anguish that she wondered if she were imagining this. It was as if the drug Gavin put in her tea on that terrible day had come to life, and, having heard its name confessed, became demonic, thrusting itself into the body of the man before her. Yet moments later, she watched his anguish dissolve into a face of compassion and sorrow, as if he were carrying the weight of everything she'd told him, as if he were straining to lift a heavy load, one too great for her to carry alone.

"I am sorry for everything I've done," she said.

The priest asked her where she was living now and what she was going to do with her life, and she told him. He asked her if she'd spoken to the authorities, if anyone had located her mother, if she had a therapist. "You've been through a very hard time," he said.

"I feel that I'll never be whole again."

Alison started to cry.

"Alison."

She wept at the sound of her name.

"God wants you to be whole and well."

"I don't know how."

"Keep coming to Mass every day. Communion is a gift from God. It will help you to forgive yourself."

She said she would try.

"For your penance, I want you to pray for those who have harmed you."

The words pushed hard into the depths of her heart like an enormous splinter. "How many times?"

"Until the pain goes away."

"That may be the rest of my life."

He paused. "We are asked to believe that God loves everyone," he said.

Alison was crying again.

He told her that God loved her and forgave her. She said an Act of Contrition, thanked him and left.

The church was empty. She knelt in a pew at the back, trying to absorb the words the priest had said to her. She would have to pray for her tormentors.

Dear God, help Wendell and Gavin to grow up.

"Love your enemies." What a stinker.

She dried her eyes and left the church.

She felt that the priest had seen into her, that he'd sensed the depth of her inarticulate suffering. Yet all he had to offer her against the danger of suicidal madness was the frailty of prayer, the hope in a God of compassion. He was a kind man. She would just have to try.

She did not know that after she left the room, the priest sat alone and prayed for her, his face in his hands.

Absent

ALISON FELT SOME RELIEF THEN, sensing in an inarticulate way that life would give her strength with every hopeful step she took. She had only two years of high school to complete, and she did well, remembering her aptitude for science and math, finding comfort in knowing what was expected of her. She began to think about her future, sharing with Maggie her childhood dream of starting life all over again, of moving to Boston, her father's city, of studying veterinary science. Her father, born of wealthy parents, had left money in trust for her, and when she turned twenty-one, it would help her begin her adult life.

She had been to Boston on a trip with her previous school as a junior entrant in a science fair, part of a team project analyzing the migratory paths of ocean birds. The team placed first. With that accomplishment in mind, she applied to a small college in the town of Newton, adjacent to Boston, and was awarded a scholarship.

"You see what you can do when you apply yourself," her mother wrote.

Once or twice a year, her mother came to Toronto to visit.

Maggie attended her high-school graduation. Her mother had a busy schedule and could not make it, but she promised Alison a special lunch on her next trip to Toronto.

Empty Glass

IN JULY, ALISON'S MOTHER CAME to the city to take her shopping for a college wardrobe. Afterwards, they had lunch at a smart café in Yorkville. Jeannette wanted to order wine, to toast to Alison's future.

"I don't drink," she said.

"Not even a sip from my glass?"

"It isn't good for me, thank you."

"You've been living with the nuns too long." Her mother ordered a small carafe of Sauvignon Blanc and an extra glass, "Just in case you change your mind," she said. Then, she told her that in two years' time, she and Wendell hoped to move to British Columbia. His teaching commitments in Montreal would be over by then, and he had applied to teach journalism at UBC.

Alison felt stung. I guess we're going our separate ways, she thought.

Her mother trained her eyes on her. "Drifting is in our DNA. I think you know that."

"Yes."

"Maybe you'll drink a toast to my happiness instead." She glanced at her empty glass.

Alison didn't.

"Do you wish me well?"

"Yes."

"So, okay. We were rotten parents," she said. "We had our troubles, your dad and I."

"Because he was gay?"

"Because we weren't cut out to be faithful."

"That must have been hard."

"It's awfully common nowadays."

"I'm never going to get married."

Her mother laughed. "You're going to become a nun?"

"I hadn't thought of it."

"With your track record, they'll never let you join."

"That's a mean dig."

"I'm sorry, dear. I should not have brought it up."

Alison said nothing. She fiddled with the wine glass, the one she'd left untouched.

"Promise me you'll go on the pill," said her mother.

"I don't have to. I told you, I'm not..."

Her mother gave her a package of condoms. "Grow up," she said.

The Butterflies

ALISON THREW THE CONDOMS in the garbage as soon as her mother was out of sight.

In her room that evening, she looked hard at the picture of her parents on her desk, beside her father's crucifix. *They will be my witnesses before God.* Then, she put her hand on her bible and promised never to have sex with anyone again. She vowed to live a humble and prayerful life, to be kind to the animals that would soon be in her care. She would be everything her mother was not.

She prayed for her mother, for Wendell, for Gavin.

Teach me how to forgive them. I don't know how.

And then she found relief.

As she lay in bed that night, she closed her eyes and saw a vision of a pair of golden butterflies bearing a fine thread as they began their painless stitchery, closing up the parts of her body that were points of entry for the joy of men.

Boston Common

WHEN SHE LEFT FOR COLLEGE in 2006, Alison would sometimes travel into Boston for a weekend, where she would attend Mass at her dad's old parish, close to the Boston Common and the Public Gardens. He used to talk about St. Bartholomew's, how they had three priests in residence in the old days when everyone in the city went to church. "Before they put the rest of the priests behind bars," said a college friend, "and before half the Catholics in town got disgusted and quit," Alison added. St. Bart's had only one priest now, a pleasant but harried pastor named Father Ron, who was often assisted in his duties by some visiting colleague in town for the weekend. He talked a lot about being inclusive, about making everyone feel welcome, so Alison decided that if she found a job in Boston, she would feel at home here.

She'd enrolled in a two-year college, so that by 2008, at age twenty-three, she'd completed her studies and found a job as a vet technician at the South Boston Animal Shelter. Over her mother's objections, she rented an apartment near work. "Why not buy a condo?" she'd asked, but Alison said, "Maybe I won't like it," when she really meant that what she wanted was a simple life with few possessions. During her first week on the job, Alison walked through the Boston Common, noticing lonely people with buggies and backpacks, homeless men and women seated on park benches, huddled in the grass.

She stopped to say hello to them. She asked them their names.

After a few moments, she could feel the stares of onlookers, hard on her back, just as they had been in Toronto, on her ragged forays to the library and ATM. Only once did she remember Gavin, his slow breath on her neck, the shiver of her body in the summer heat.

She got up and left.

The Falcon Ought to Have a Name

ALISON FELT AT HOME IN BOSTON, but having grown up in Toronto, where most cars stopped for red lights, she would panic as she crossed Park Street and Tremont, or Boylston or Mass Avenue. "The cars don't *want* to stop, do they," she said to her boss, who explained that the squirrel population had discovered this long ago but hadn't learned a thing from their discovery.

She loved working with animals, providing care and comfort, giving them medications and vaccines and X-rays and blood tests, discussing their conditions with their human companions. She let her job absorb her life the way sunlight blots up the last muddy patches of winter snow.

Once a week, she emailed her mother to tell her how life was progressing. She enjoyed doing this. It made her feel like a normal person with a family; it made her forget that she had ever lived on the street. Her correspondence allowed her to join in conversations about families at work, when in her high-school days, boarding with nuns — and even later, in college — she'd avoided the subject altogether. Her mother's response was usually, "So glad you're happy, So glad you're making friends, etc." Alison accepted the fact that her mother didn't have much to say to her. The life between them, frayed and torn, dangled by a frail thread, and Alison felt this to be her fault, as much as her mother's. She also emailed Maggie, keeping her posted on the progress of her new life.

St. Bartholomew's Church was close to the Common so in good weather, she would go to Mass before work. She was in Boston a few months when she noticed a new visiting priest, a trim, blue-eyed man, his blond hair lashed with silver, a man who, despite his evident fitness, wore a look of profound spiritual exhaustion.

As she walked down the aisle to receive Communion, Alison felt his eyes on her as she approached him, saw the cloud of sorrow lift from his face, and for a moment, it seemed as if she were bringing him the Eucharist: something unexpected by way of refreshment.

Puzzled, she left for work after Mass with the priest on her mind. Later that day, a cop pulled into the South Boston Animal Shelter with an injured fledgling, a falcon with a broken wing. She prepped the raptor for surgery, rested a hand on its breast to give it what comfort she could, and feeling the warmth of the frightened creature and its beating heart, she remembered how she herself had been rescued from death by a woman named Marguerite who called herself Maggie, who knelt beside her and called her name. She thought then that this poor falcon ought to have a name, as it already did in the heart of God.

It was a female. She would name it for Marguerite, who rescued her.

Hers was the French name for a flower.

Daisy.

Peregrines

Fine Porcelain

IT WAS 2011. MORE THAN A YEAR had passed since Daisy had come into her life, and eight years had fled since Gavin's savage attack. Her sorrow was a vanished river running deep underground, its current strong enough to shape her inner world. She missed her lost father who was still a living presence, while her mother had become nothing more than a lifelong struggle with forgiveness. Of those who realized what had happened to her, all of them lived in Toronto — Maggie, her therapist, and the parish priest who had offered her compassion.

It was because of them that she stitched together a garment of faith, sufficient to warm her in the chill of life. In the Cross, she saw an image of the pain that never ended on this broken earth, and in the blessings of life and beauty, she saw rescue. Her father had believed that in the mystery of this earth, all God's creatures were beloved. She took comfort in that.

Apart from this, there was no solace for what had happened to her.

Now in her twenties, she was a child with a stone heart; her insides burned with shock, as if she'd been tampered with by a wet finger in a light socket. She sensed that she would never grow beyond this, that she conveyed to others — especially Cam and Father Matt — that there was something wrong with her. She tried to make friends, but beyond Daisy, she had no desire for a life companion. It was spring now, but she felt brittle, like fine porcelain veined with cracks, easy to smash with a careless brush of the hand.

Now, after all of that, they were going to close the church.

From: alison@sbas.com
To: cameraman@fordhamu.edu
Re: St. Bart's closing
Date: 1 March 2011

Hi Cam,
You may not know this, but St. Bart's is closing. They lost a lot of parishioners when street people started coming to the church for Mass and the parish ran out of money. I should never have taken Daisy into the park because that's how the whole thing started. I used to go with her to sit and visit with the homeless people along with some parishioners and then Matt came and celebrated Mass with them. He did it all last summer and into the fall, and when it got cold, they came into the church. Father Matt is devastated. He does not look well.
Alison

From: cameraman@fordhamu.edu
To: Alison@sbas.com
Re: St. Bart's closing
Date: 1 March 2011

Alison, I hadn't heard about St. Bart's. You're not at fault for this. You and Matt were doing something good in the park. I know it's sad, but the heart can only break in so many pieces. Be gentle with yourself. BTW, I am going to be in Boston for a series of weekends in April and May, teaching an ecotheo course at Boston College. Hope we can touch base.
Cam

Not Her Fault

THERE WAS A FRAMED PHOTO in Matt's office that he prized as one of his favourites. It showed him standing beside his mother on his ordination day. He looked young and confident, his gaze alight with hope, a radiant second caught by the camera, a lightness he prayed would not be tarnished by the passing years. He did some counselling out of his office at St. Bart's, and he put the photo there to remind him of his calling, of the reality of hope for himself and others. Alison had commented on it more than once. "We're so brave when we're young," she'd said. Unable to sleep, Matt found himself reflecting on the photo. He wasn't sure how to think about the closing of St. Bart's. He was only there to help out, and then he found himself entangled in Alison's haunted world, in her wayfarer's walk with Daisy that had led him into the park. He wondered if it were possible that Alison had dragged him — and the whole parish, in fact — into the net of a waking dream that possessed her. Pretty outrageous speculation, he realized. Yet it was not impossible to consider the power of that woman who, as Father Ron had reported, had drawn a following of so many parishioners, her and her Pied Piper falcon. He'd gone along with it; they all had.

Except that it wasn't her fault. He and Ron had liked the thought of community involvement and the big-deal buzzwords of "inclusiveness," and "reaching out to the marginalized," and Alison (with Daisy attached) had approached her park companions with a natural grace that captivated everyone. And in the end, it was Alison who'd confronted his flagging grip on reality, his thought that he might live among the homeless, that he might minister to them. He would never forget the glint of steel in her voice.

"There's no good way to live on the street," she said.

"Not among the poor?"

"Not among insults and very sick men and women. No."

"I feel at home with them," said Matt.

"That is not the same as living among them. I will do nothing to support this," said Alison. Her voice sliced the air, her eyes flashing with a bright, metallic fury. Matt had never seen her defiant, never imagined she had it in her.

"That man with the wine — John — he's full of contempt for you."

"Not for me. For the priest who molested him."

"But you're not that priest, and there's no reason to let him poison you," she said. "No one else will drink that wine."

Matt was silent, and then he spoke.

"I will continue to say Mass in the park," he said.

Alison was fine with that.

John is full of contempt for you. He couldn't deny it.

Yet he felt drawn to the men and women on the Common. John, Bill, Pete, Tommy, Flora. He didn't know why; it was as if he had encountered them in some past life, a thought quite foreign — and not at all agreeable — to his priestly training. It felt as if these people were tapping on his shoulder, trying to tell him he'd neglected something, only he could not for the life of him name what it was; nothing more than one of those frustrating thoughts that circles the drain and slips through the strainer of old age. He would give this painful occlusion of his soul to God, he thought. Their suffering and his, held in the blessing of stale bread and sour wine. Their hope of rebirth, drunk to the dregs.

He belonged there.

Their Son

MATT SAID MASS IN THE PARK the following morning, and as he prayed, he looked out over the edge of the crowd and saw a slender, bearded man with ebony skin and a red-haired woman wheeling a baby stroller. Then he remembered the email he'd neglected to answer: "Dear Matt, I have obtained a position teaching theology at Boston College and Natalie and I will be moving back here." He had received it … when? Six weeks, six months ago? He couldn't remember.

He did not look or feel well, and he didn't want them to spot him. He hoped they'd move on, and they continued on their walk.

When Mass was done, and he had drunk the remains of John's wine, he looked up to see Elias, a tall tree-trunk of a man leaning into the bright sky, and Natalie, red-gold hair undulating in the breeze, her body like a dancer's, as if he were viewing her reflection in water, and then a child in a stroller. They said hello to him, looked at him with concern in their eyes, joined him on the bench long enough for Natalie to introduce their six-month-old son. His name was James Andre, after her late uncle and his partner — and, according to Nigerian custom, a repertoire of family names were also attached to the common ones, so that he became the engine of his father's clan moving through time, transporting its cargo of riches to America. Matt did not know what to say. He felt part of that clan, in memory of the man who was his son.

Elias gave him a card with his address and phone number, and they asked what he was up to, and he told them, "A new ministry." Elias patted his shoulder. "Father, you have chosen the narrow path," he said. "Do not tire yourself."

Natalie asked him for his email address, and he wrote it down, relieved that he was composed enough to do her that courtesy. "You must come for supper, just like old times," said Natalie, the cook, whose uncle had slept with the man who'd turned out to be his rejected son.

Natalie, whose worried face said more than her words.

Something's On His Mind

NATALIE EYED A YOUNG WOMAN, a falcon on her gloved fist. "Oh my goodness. Is that Alison from the chat room?"

Matt told her that it was. "You should speak to her," he said.

Suspecting that Matt was too tired for conversation, Natalie and Elias introduced themselves to Alison.

"Such a proud-looking creature," said Elias as he eyed Daisy with care. He told Alison that his was a family of falconers, and he asked if he might hold the bird. Alison gave him a glove and the tethers and Daisy made herself comfortable on his arm. The three of them walked around the Common, stroller and bird in hand, attracting stares, talking about the chat room.

Alison mentioned that Cameron Byrne would be in town soon. Maybe they could all get together. Little James kept stretching his pudgy hands toward Daisy.

"Will you bring Daisy over to visit?" asked Natalie.

Alison promised she would.

Elias lowered his voice. "How is Father Matt?" he asked.

"He's working too hard," she said. "Coming up to Easter. Something's on his mind, but I'm not sure what."

Useless Clutter

ALISON KNEW NATALIE AND ELIAS from the chat room, so she felt comfortable babysitting James, carting Daisy over to their house in the used van she'd just bought for her Raptor Education gigs in the schools. It was a busy time; Cam was coming to town in early April, and with the church getting ready to close, Father Ron had asked the parishioners to organize a book sale to dispose of the contents of the parish library. Alison had volunteered to help.

Around that time, she received an email from her mother announcing that she and Wendell were moving to Vancouver at last. "I'm busy throwing out junk and useless clutter," she wrote. "I've perused a small cache of your dad's papers. I'll send them along for you in case you'd like to keep them. If not, feel free to shred them."

Alison felt a pang of sadness. "Junk and useless clutter," her dad's papers. At least she's giving me a chance to look at them, she thought.

A few days later, the parcel arrived. Inside was a folder full of papers, each one dated, all dates in order from first to last. They appeared to be copies of letters that her father had written and sent from 1992 to 1995, the year of his death. Clipped to each was a reply. "Dearest Edward," the first one began.

And the second.

And the third.

Love letters. I should not be reading them, she thought. *He's dead. Does it matter?*

Her mother, she realized, must have read them all.

She remembered that not long after her unpleasant encounter with Princess the hawk, Edward disappeared from their lives. Then she began to read, recoiling in shock as if she were holding a rifle that had fired without warning.

"My Dear Edward," the last letter read. "...I can't continue in this way. My love for you is in profound conflict with my love for the Catholic faith...."

Alison felt nauseated and disgusted all at once. I can't read this, I can't, she thought. But she knew if she didn't, she would never find out what happened. She continued reading.

> *...My conscience won't accept the duplicity of my life. I love you, but I feel that I should restrain myself, that I should be your friend, but not your lover. I've been deceitful. I've forced my wife into unfaithfulness. I've been inattentive to my daughter's needs. I am betraying the faith that asks of us a certain forbearance in the sufferings that life puts in our path.... I know you will not understand. I know that today's youth think differently about these things, but you are much younger than I am, and I have been formed differently. I'm distressed by the truth that I began this relationship, and that in approaching you, I've broken every vow I've ever made.... I love you and I will pray for you, but I no longer want to see you.*
> *With love, Paul*

There was no response attached to this letter. *My poor father. He could not forgive himself, and it killed him.* She felt soiled by reading what was none of her business — and that, she realized, had made her feel nauseous and disgusted, along with the realization that her father would have been better off embracing a more benign idea of faith, one that would have helped him to leave her mother and love Edward. Dizzy, she lay down, afraid she'd faint. In an instant, she understood that the kindly father she'd carried in her heart, the man whose gentle voice had guided her through her wanderings was gone forever, replaced by the image of a grief-stricken, tormented man. One soul, yes, but the two images would not converge. Her brain refused to give her eyes the wholeness of that man.

He loved birds. Once, he was a falconer.

What am I going to do with all of this?

Her mother's words: "I'll send them along for you in case you'd like to keep them."

What a rotten thing to do, she thought. The steaming rot of a sewer.

I'm drinking from a clear stream, and you come along and dump the sewage in.

What the hell is the matter with you?

I'm From the Bronx

THERE ARE TIMES, THOUGHT ALISON, when you should not bear witness. *I have already seen too much of my parents' lives.*

Her phone rang. It was Cam, who had just arrived in town. She told him about her mother's leaving for Vancouver with her boyfriend, starting a new life, unloading her father's papers, and saying *toodle-oo.*

"Excuse me, but what a piece of shit. She's your *mother.*"

Alison was surprised. She had not expected this blunt response, and she told him that.

"I'm from the Bronx," he said.

She mentioned that her father's correspondence was far too personal for her to read.

"And your mother *sent* you that?"

"He was a gay man, and they were love letters."

"You were supposed to read them?"

"My dad and I were close."

"Not *that* close."

"That," she said, "is what I'm going to tell my mother."

Cold Hands

BRAVE WORDS, SHE THOUGHT as she hung up the phone. She couldn't go back on them. Cam would ask her how her mother had reacted. She sat down at the computer and began her email.

From: Alison@sbas.com
To: jeannette@photog.com
Re: letters
Date: April 15, 2011

I read one of Dad's letters, and I'm wondering why you wanted me to read them. They were never meant to be read by me, I am certain. They were far too personal, and I don't need to know more than the fact that Dad was gay. Since you don't want those letters, I am going to shred them.

Alison paused, thought a minute, then finished the email.

By the way, I'm not going to call you Jeannette anymore. Quit holding me at arm's-length like a smelly sock. Either you're my mother or you're not.

Before sending it, she went to cross herself, then stopped, feeling her hands cold with fury, every blessing wrung out of them.

The hell with it, she thought. *Pray for your goddamn self, Mom.*

She hit "Send."

Frailty

A DAY PASSED, AND HER MOTHER responded. When Alison clicked on the subject line, the page was blank. Glitch, she thought. *She'll try again.*

She didn't.

A week passed.

Maybe she's disappeared. Or is in the process of disappearing with her lover. If I were to see them in Montreal, on Rue Ste. Catherine, I might peer through them, see restaurants and sidewalk cafés greyed out against a floating membrane, a placenta detached from the life of a child, the ripple of a sheer veil pulled across reality.

But I am the one who cannot see. I have let go of them. I am no longer capable of reading my mother's words. They are invisible, written in a language I refuse to speak, a language of I-need-her-I-love-her-it-was-all-my-fault-forgive-me. It is I who am disappearing from her world.

Perhaps she cannot read my messages.

Perhaps no one can see me anymore.

The truth is that all of us will vanish.

A week ago, I was sorting books in the rectory, and Father Matt told me the sad story of how he came to love birds. He is also frail. He carries within him unfathomable shock and loss from the flight he missed that destroyed so many. So, I spoke to him about the gifts of the hawk, the falcon, the spirituality of these creatures, their embodiment of mystery.

What I did not tell him was that since adopting Daisy, I have learned that in falconry lore, an aggressive name for the raptor will produce a passive creature. So, no Genghis Khans, no Stalins or Napoleons. They will never hunt for you. If you want a killer, name your falcon ... Daisy. Yet my Daisy is not like that. Perhaps if she could hunt, she would be fierce, but if the gentle carry fire, then Daisy bears the flame of the Holy Spirit.

I am remembering my father's prayer.

"I am a transient being, homeless, and God is my shelter."

"I will lift up a falcon, a fiery torch to light the way home."

As for me, I am as frail as my parents, a crockery vase with a hollow centre and a thousand tiny cracks. I did not deserve the horror that was done to me, and yet it happened. This is the fate of human clay, broken soul and heart, bones in a shroud, waiting for a thunderclap, the stone rolled back.

A Bad Read

GOD BLESS CAM. HE'S SO BLUNT, got me off my butt around my mother, she thought. Cam was in town to give a few classes. He had invited her to sit in on his Saturday session, but she had promised to help sort books for the parish sale. With the weight of her mother gone, she felt lighter, as if she had unloaded an unwieldy backpack. Today's task would be mundane, but she enjoyed perusing old tomes, even the musty and neglected fare stashed in a parish library. After so poignant an encounter with her father's writing, she welcomed the relief of tired prose.

Alison put Daisy in her cage and took her to the church, hoping she would not be irritated by the dust and mould of so many unread books. "Yes, Daisy does sneeze from time to time," she tells school kids, "although sneezes usually follow eating." Having never exposed her to dust, Alison had no idea how she might react.

The parish library doubled as Father Matt's office. The door had been left unlocked, and she went in with the cage. Matt wasn't there, but her eye caught the striking photo taken on the day of his ordination, and she thought that the luminous image of Matt was company enough. She had wanted to work alone since she'd left the office in some disarray, with stacks of books on the floor, in open boxes.

Within the hour, Matt showed up. He looked frazzled, impaled on a bolt of lightning. *Frizzled and fried.* She asked if he needed anything, if she were in the way.

"No problem," he said, but she knew there was.

She continued sorting books in silence, while Matt worked on the opposite side of the room, tossing bulletins and out-of-date periodicals in the recycle bin with ballistic efficiency that signalled equal parts distress and fury. Alison felt uncomfortable. Then she spotted a slim book, Matt hurling it with a pitcher's aim, a curveball thrown from across the room that sent the unwanted volume over his desk and *thunk*, straight into the bin, pages bent and cover askew, visible evidence of a rotten read.

"Ball one," said Alison. Matt didn't smile.

"I'll take care of the bin," he said.

"It must have been a terrible book."

"It is evidence that priests make stupid errors in judgment, just like everyone else," said Matt.

Alison walked over to the bin and peered at the cover. The book was face down and she couldn't see the author's name.

"Not good enough for the sale?" she asked. "People buy all kinds of..."

"They won't be buying this one." He paused. "Have a look, if you like."

She took the book out of the bin, then gasped and dropped it.

"What's wrong?"

"Who is this author? The name is..."

" ...no one you'd want to know."

"But the name is ... tell me who it is."

"You can't read it?" Matt looked alarmed.

"I can't." She panicked. Letters strung together, but she was unable to make sense of the words. She grabbed the edge of Matt's desk.

"Sit down, Alison."

She did. She felt faint.

"Are you all right?" he asked.

"It's nothing." Her heart was racing. She'd dropped the book so that it was face down, so that the author's photo on the back was visible.

She couldn't speak. Matt got her a glass of water.

"Is he famous?" she said at last because she knew who it was and didn't know what else to say.

"Infamous," said Matt. "He did time for drugs, and his book came out last year."

"Did you…"

"His dad's a hotshot in Toronto," said Matt. "Big college donor. Set him up for a book-signing. Last year, when I was teaching at St. Mike's. Natalie and Elias wouldn't go."

"And you?"

"I thought he'd surely reformed. He said that my work had inspired him."

"But you didn't like the book."

Matt paused. "He never changed. He preys on homeless women. Now he's…"

The rest of the sentence crumbled in his mouth.

Alison grew pale. She saw that her strong body, its health restored, began to evaporate before his eyes.

Matt kept looking at her.

Shy Young Man

EIGHT YEARS OF TIME AND MEMORY dissolved into a warm September in 2003, with a quick trip to Toronto for an academic conference, the conclusion of a students' welcome Mass at St. Basil's church, and him about to lunch with the college president, along with corporate lawyer Duncan Moore. The man's son, Gavin, stopped by to speak with them, a young man with the kind of classic features found in museum statuary, whose introverted gaze seemed focused on a great, invisible mirror. He did not look like today's student. He dressed like an old boy from Upper Canada College: tailored shirt, V-neck sweater, and tie. Matt liked him. He seemed like a gentleman, all courtesy and deference. He hearkened back to a sedate and cultivated world, one he wished he could claim, so far from the troubles of his own youth. Matt had not yet met him; that would come seven years later. And Gavin had not yet been in trouble with the law, had not yet mistaken Matt's office for the Men's Room.

Then, out of the church, came a young woman dressed in shabby jeans and jacket, hair askew, lugging a tattered backpack that protruded from her body like an enormous growth. She seemed incoherent (or so he thought), her gaze too purposeless to be a student's, her face marked with the pallor and hollowed cheeks of a substance abuser. He hated to be so callous; he sensed that he was reacting to her for punching a hole through the fair skies of a late-summer day, one in which he relished his position, the respect and achievement he had earned for himself. The woman's eyes would not connect with his (drugs would do that); she handed him an envelope, saying that she wanted prayers (reminding him, he supposed, that he was a priest after all, with duties other than dining out). Yes, there are destitute people in this world, but there are also parasites, he'd thought. Then, as she turned to leave, Gavin pulled out his camera and took her picture.

"Do you know her?" Matt asked.

"Not at all. I do this now and again. I collect photos. I don't actually..."

"What will you do with it?" He wondered if he was doing research for a thesis.

"I guess I like her. Do you think she'd talk to me?"

Matt remembered feeling a trace of alarm at the way Gavin's mood swerved from a rather chilly collector of women's photos to a man who wanted to pursue his subject. Quit psychoanalyzing everything, he thought. Gavin was a shy young man, that's all.

Matt shrugged. "No harm in trying," he said, then paused. "I noticed she took Communion."

"I watched her all during Mass," said Gavin.

"So go for it," Matt said.

To his surprise, Gavin took off down the path, after the young woman.

He can't be for real, he thought.

Matt opened the envelope that the woman had given him. He pulled out a slip of paper, a note written in pencil. It was almost illegible. He crumpled it up and threw it in a trash bin.

Photo

ALISON WAITED FOR FATHER MATT to speak. She sensed his hesitation.

"Gavin Moore's been charged with rape."

Alison hid her face in her hands.

Matt sighed. "These things are hard to talk about."

"How awful."

"Natalie's mother sent her a link to *The Star*. He preyed on street kids, had a thing about taking their photos, posting them on social media. That's how they caught him." He paused. "That's why his book's in the bin."

Alison reached for her handbag, pulled out her father's prayer book and withdrew a folded piece of paper.

"He took a photo at St. Basil's Church," she said. "September, 2003."

Matt's heart turned to ice.

"He sent it to me. I printed it off his email."

She opened the paper and handed it to Matt.

Ashes

MATT STARED AT THE PHOTO of the waif, thin as a dime, haunted eyes, and hair askew, her swollen hump of a backpack, her gaze confused and innocent. How easy it would be to prey on a child like this. He looked up to see Alison's face, wet with tears.

She dried her eyes. "The following day, he came after me."

"I didn't know you were..."

"I lived in the ravine. He gave me the photo. Every day, he brought me books to read. He waited two months." She mentioned drugs, then what he'd done.

"Did you tell the police?"

"No. It was just too shameful."

She told him about her recovery, how she decided to start life again in her dad's hometown, how she saw Matt at Mass.

"But you didn't recognize me," she said.

"No," he said. "No, Alison, I did not."

"I had to bulk up for Vet Tech."

"Please forgive me, Alison," he said. "Gavin wanted to follow you that day at church. I didn't stop him." He said no more, overwhelmed with remorse at what he'd set in motion.

Alison let herself cry.

Confession

"IF I NEED A SHRINK, it won't be you," Gavin had said.

Over a year ago, Matt wondered how he had known Gavin, if he might have heard Gavin's confession. The thought filled him with dread.

"You were very forgiving," said Gavin.

He wondered what he'd meant by that. Now he began to imagine what Gavin might have confessed, which made the thought of it all the more terrible. Something like: "I seduced a woman who came to my house."

"Did you know her?"

"Not well. Street kid. She needed a place to wash up, so I offered her my home. I knew I made a mistake, the minute I let her in. She was beautiful, all cleaned up."

"You must learn to think clearly. The law doesn't take kindly to these situations."

"I'm really sorry. I want to improve my life. I don't want to disappoint my parents."

Gavin would never have admitted that he raped her. Gavin had been playing games with him. Nothing more.

He wondered now why the man would have bothered to confess in the first place. Or why he himself had bothered to conjure it up. And yet, in his imagined scenario, he had cast Gavin as a gentleman and Alison as a side issue, no more than a young man's failure at self-improvement.

Bookmark

WHEN SHE LEFT THE DISARRAY of Father Matt's office, Alison shut the door and noticed a prayer card that had slipped through the space between the door and the floor. She picked it up. On it was an image of the cross surrounded by lilies. Father Matt must have tossed it out in a frenzy, no doubt a bookmark in some outdated periodical or even Gavin Moore's work. She felt that the image, so redolent of sorrow redeemed by hope, had, in some providential way, been meant for her consolation. *Father Matt doesn't need this.* She slipped it in her pocket.

All That Glass

THAT EVENING, SHE SAT WITH DAISY on her gloved fist. "Daisy, how do I forgive him?" She was still crying.

The falcon turned her vast and beautiful eyes toward her, and Alison wondered at her powerful beak and talons, her wings that would lift but never fly again.

If Daisy could think, she would have to forgive God.

Or maybe us, for building all those towers, all that glass that she mistook for sky.

A blessing, not to think so hard. Life is so terrible, in every sense.

How I wish for the wisdom of the birds.

70 x 7

MATT KNEW WHAT HIS OWN CONFESSOR was going to say. "'You must forgive not seven times, but seventy-seven times.' You know the gospel. So does she. If she doesn't forgive you, it's not your problem." Legalism, he thought. What priests let each other get away with, around harmless and vulnerable women.

"Did you touch her?"

"No, of course not."

"Did you have immoral thoughts? Did you take any pleasure in thinking them?"

"No on both counts."

"So relax."

He had been forgiven more times than he deserved. Of course, he had nothing to do with Gavin's crimes, his choice to do harm. But there was that cronyism known to priests and to their male friends in power, an invisible pollutant that fouled the air, an unwitting exclusion of all who tried, like that brave young girl, to make their presence known. He could have helped her — he who had rejected a woman's love, who had been brought to the point of death by drugs, who had been shown such kindness and compassion. Instead, he had buddied up to Gavin and sent an indifferent message, delivered with a shrug.

"So, go for it," he had said.

Gavin was a rapist.

He himself had once killed an innocent man.

Prayer Card

YET MATT WANTED AT LEAST the solace of prayer. He looked for his breviary and couldn't find it. *Lord, I'm getting careless.* Then, he noticed a heap of abandoned books and papers on the floor, and there he found the prayer book, dumped in a careless moment, headed for the recycle bin. *I'm losing it.* It was a gift for his ordination, years ago, with ribbon markers, a different colour for each liturgical season. No way to treat such a precious book.

It had also contained a prayer card, old and worn. *In Memory of Andre Lefèvre.*

He flipped through the pages, looking for it.

Gone. It may have ended up in the recycle bin.

He spent the rest of the morning, searching.

Phone Message

ALISON HAD BEEN INVITED to bring Daisy to a raptor display on Easter Sunday, as part of a family event at the Boston Nature Center. It was, she realized, a legitimate way of avoiding Father Matt at the noon Mass.

Yet Natalie and Elias had organized an Easter dinner for that evening because Cam was in town, a kind of theological chat room reunion (with special treats for Daisy), and both she and Father Matt had been invited. She would have to make the best of that. It was the shock of what Matt revealed about Gavin, that's all, she thought.

She still felt raw, as if these revelations had flayed her, had peeled skin back from the body of memory. Yet she was grateful for the friendship of Natalie and Elias, for the way in which they included her in their family. She would do her best to enjoy the dinner, to focus on the chat room, on news about Armande and Josephine and the hawklets.

When she returned home on Easter Sunday, she had phone messages from Natalie and Cam. "Please call asap."

My Heart Is Old

CAMERON FOUND OUT ABOUT Matt's heart attack from Elias who'd been at the noon Mass, who'd been worried ever since he'd driven Matt home from dinner a week or so ago. The man didn't look well, he told Natalie; he never took time off. Natalie logged on to the chat room, so that now the entire group knew about Matt's collapse in the sacristy.

Alison answered phone messages from both Natalie and Cam. "How terrible," was all she could manage to say to Natalie. "Is he going to live?"

"It's under control," Nat told her. "Come over, Allie, we've got lots of food. We'll talk."

"He'll pull through," said Cam, and she felt in his tone of voice the assurance that it would be so.

With Daisy in tow, she had Easter dinner with Natalie, Elias, their son James, and Cam. It was still early when they left, and Cam asked Alison if she and Daisy would like to go for a stroll in the Public Garden. "Walk off some of this excellent food," he said.

Alison hadn't eaten much. She felt pensive, afraid of the air that touched her skin, afraid of her own words. When they got to the park, Cam asked her if she had told her mother off.

"I did," said Alison. "She responded with a blank page."

"This I gotta see."

"I said I wouldn't call her 'Jeannette' anymore."

"Huh?"

"That's her name. I wasn't allowed to call her 'Mom.'"

"Sheesh."

"It doesn't matter now. That blank page means she's disappeared."

"To you, anyway."

She looked away. "I carry her in my bones," she said. "I can't get rid of my parents."

Cam was quiet. "You're also God's child," he said at last.

"I know that," she answered. "But God didn't bring me up."

He turned to her, felt Daisy's eye on him, took her free hand in both of his. "Alison," he said. "They made you so unhappy."

"I came to Boston to have a new life."

He let go of her hand. "I'm getting too personal," he said.

"It's hard to talk about." She found a tissue and dabbed at her eyes.

"I didn't mean to pry."

"Father Matt had a heart attack because he knew too much about it." Daisy pecked at her damp cheek.

"How do you mean?"

"Someone has to know this," she whispered, as if she were alone.

"Know what, Allie?"

It was because she trusted Cam that she let her words fall on the parched ground of silence, drenching it like a deep and steady rain. She told Cam how her good father died, how her home life dissolved in grief, how she fell into the arms of a man Cam's age, how she ended up on the street. She related what Matt had revealed in his office.

Then she told him what Gavin had done to her.

Cam was silent.

"I wanted the snow to bury me alive," she said. "I can't forget it."

Even the birds were still.

"I didn't mean to cry," she said. "I'm sorry."

"It's all right, Allie."

The two of them sat, as quiet as the evening.

"And you're so young," he said at last.

"My heart is old."

"Mine, too," he replied, head bowed.

The Broken Sky

After this conversation, we walked at dusk, circling the Public Garden, its fountains and swan boats and charming bridge, the tulips and daffodils in bloom, Daisy drawing stares and smiles, and it was still Easter, and Cam took my free hand again and said, "Remember when I promised to be your friend?" and I said, "Yes, and you said you'd never ask anything more of me and I said that we all need friends."

Then he told me that I'd seemed so frightened, that he hoped I was no longer frightened of him. I told him no, but it worried me to think where this might be going, and then he said, "I appreciate your company, Alison. I told you my son was your age when he died in Iraq and I lost my wife to leukemia. Both of them left this world too soon, but I am consoled ... I find you so refreshing."

He paused, turned to me, put his hands on my shoulders, and then I knew I had to tell him the truth. "Cam," I said, "I've taken a vow of celibacy."

He looked surprised. "Are you entering religious life?" he asked.

"No," I said.

"Then why?"

"Because sex almost destroyed me, and I don't want the life

that my mother led, and then there was the rape."

"Before whom did you make this vow?" he asked, and I told him that I'd made it before God, and I saw that his eyes were wet.

"I promise not to take advantage, but God won't, either," said Cam. "If you meet a young man who loves you, don't be afraid to return that love."

"In the end we will be judged by love." It was his favourite saying of Saint John of the Cross, but I wanted to tell him that I would never be able to love a young man because Gavin treated me even worse than Wendell, and then Cam asked if he could just put his arm around my shoulders and we would still be friends and that was all he wanted.

I was grateful for Daisy, perched between us with fierce beak and talons, because I might have forgotten my vow, and I said it was okay, he could put his arm around my shoulders, and then I remembered last summer when he came to give a lecture at the church and I saw the broken sky inside of him.

Now with him pressing against me, what I felt were two savage wounds, two pieces of shattered glass that did not fit together to form a whole, their sharp edges puncturing each other's skin. We were both desperate enough to allow this, to go further in the falling darkness, but I pulled away and told him I could not.

Insights

MY FATHER TOOK A VOW *of celibacy, then died of grief.*
It was not my fear of the hawk that killed him.
Am I going to die like this?

Loneliness is killing Father Matt.
It is killing all of us.

Forgiveness

AFTER MATT WAS RELEASED from the hospital, Alison wrote him a letter. She felt that her message was too important for email.

Dear Fr. Matt,

I hope you are feeling better and that you will take as long as you need to get well.

Here is what I would like you to know. You asked me to forgive you. Life has taught me that forgiveness happens bit by bit, and time allows it room to grow.

We both received a terrible shock on that day when we spoke. I think you know that.

I hope you will forgive yourself. As for me, I have been writing about my early life, allowing forgiveness some room to breathe. When I am ready to share my written thoughts with you, then you'll know that you are forgiven.

Get well soon,

Alison

Alone

MATT WAS AT SHOREHAVEN, recuperating from his heart attack in the late spring of 2011. He avoided vacationers, went for walks, read, did some writing, celebrated Mass. A kind parishioner drove him to cardiac rehab. He prayed and took walks. He'd had occasional visits from Elias and Natalie and baby James, and from Father Ron. Alison wrote him a letter on stationery depicting a robin on her nest, with the requisite three blue eggs and flowering branch. It was a generous letter. She said she was trying to forgive him.

Company

Life has been easier this spring. Natalie has been teaching me how to cook. Elias loves Daisy and falconry in general, and I like spending time with little Jamie. On Sunday evenings, we have dinner together. On Tuesday evenings, I go to meetings with a group of graduate students that Cam brought together when he taught here in April. He had invited me to bring Daisy to their seminar, and they asked me if I'd like to join their Orni-theology group (Ornithology Plus). Yes, we do theology by reflecting on bird life. We read Teilhard de Chardin, Thomas Berry, and the Peterson Field Guide. *Also Cam's* The Birds of the Air. *Since it's May, we have spent some weekend time together, observing migratory birds. The members of the group invited me to join them for a boat trip out of Provincetown this summer — whale-watching, but with an eye for seabirds which I've never seen. It feels different here without Father Matt. In some ways, better. I am spending much less time alone. Daisy and I are exploring the pleasures of human company.*

They Don't Care

THE NAMES, TO ALISON'S MIND, were beautiful: storm petrel, great shearwater, northern gannet, pomerine jaeger. Pelagic birds that roam the seas and breed on distant islands; they were the poetry of things imagined, hope unseen. It was July, and she had made it to Provincetown. Five years in Boston, and she had just begun to explore the old settlement at the tip of the Cape, its frame houses brilliant with flowers, its narrow streets crowded and alive. She was happy to be away from Boston, to feel the sea breeze against her skin as she made her way to the dock.

Natalie and Elias had rented a cottage in nearby Truro, and Alison had asked them if they would look after Daisy while she headed north for the whale-watching trip. She planned to call Father Matt before she drove back to Boston, stopping by Shorehaven if he felt well enough to see her. When she dropped off Daisy, Natalie invited her to stay over and leave in the morning.

"Matt hasn't wanted visitors," said Natalie. "He says he needs time to himself."

"He is not happy," said Elias. "His superior wants him to go on a retreat when he is well. It is likely he will not return to Boston."

Alison was puzzled. "What about his teaching?"

"They don't care about teaching. They care about the homeless

Mass," said Natalie. "And the church closing. They care about obedience. He stepped out of line on the Common. They told him to cut it out and he wouldn't. That, and being famous and getting too big for his boots. That's how they see it."

"He's just ... lonely."

Alison felt their eyes on her.

"It's the way he lives," said Alison. "He doesn't know how to connect."

"I've been saying that for years," said Natalie.

Elias looked pensive. "He has a degree in psych," he began. "But he misses so many things."

"Yeah, and he was shocked when that prick got charged with rape," said Natalie. "I sure wasn't. Did he tell you guys about that?"

Alison murmured, "A bit." She thanked them for looking after Daisy, told them she'd be on her way.

What Good

MATT HAD RECEIVED A VISIT from his superior on the previous day, and the man described his order's plans for him. He was not going to contest them, understanding, as he did now, that his desire to be among the lost souls of the Common was nothing more than conscience gripping him by the collar, tugging at his muddled thoughts, kicking him in the shins and yelling into his deaf ears, "*Look what you let happen to that girl. You could have gotten help for her. You could have sent her to a safe place, but you were not of a mind to do that. You let that young man prey on her. You saw it in his eyes. All those omissions you carried with you to the Common, and that's why you let John the wino mock you and insult you. Penance not ministry. And what good did it do?*"

He could not answer that question. Yet earlier that summer, Alison had sent him some of her writing, her reflections on her early life. "When I am ready to share my written thoughts with you, then you'll know that you are forgiven." At least he had that much. *Forgive me, Alison.* He did not feel he deserved more.

Cape Fog

ALISON HAD NOT SEEN MATT in the three months that had passed since his heart attack, but when she called him, he said she was welcome to come. He sounded formal — what you might expect of a priest who had never met you. Or, sad to say, even one who had.

He's not feeling well, that's the reason.

I don't have to stay long, she thought.

She felt refreshed after the cruise, after seeing the magnificent birds as they criss-crossed the waves in the crash and sparkle of sunlight, after watching a pod of whales playing and leaping and spouting along the side of the boat, after sharing the thrill with five men and women her own age, along with a crowd of excited families. She didn't want to tarnish that experience.

After the trip, she drove to Truro to pick up Daisy, and then to the south side of Shorehaven, to the rectory.

Matt looked as grey as a Cape fog. His hair had grown white and his trim frame slack and thin. He seemed frail, no longer sturdy and fit. They sat outside, on the rectory's patio facing the shore. She asked him how he was feeling.

"Believe it or not, I'm on the mend," he said. "I hope you're well."

She told him about the birding trip with Cam's students.

"Cam's too old for you."

"Cam wasn't there." She felt annoyed, then puzzled at his

state of mind. Matt seemed a bit dazed, as if he were speaking to someone else.

He asked how Daisy was.

Alison put on her glove and opened the door of her cage. "C'mon, Daisy. Let's pay Father Matt a visit," she said.

Matt watched in silence as Daisy rose and flexed her wings. "May I hold her?" he asked.

Holding Daisy

GAZING AT THE FALCON, Matt had felt as if the creature were blessed for a moment with the gift of perception. What do you know about the world to come, my friend? Matt thought.

"Only God knows," said an inner voice.

Feeling certain that Daisy had heard that same inner voice, Matt had felt prompted to ask Alison if he might hold the falcon.

"Of course," Alison had said, her face registering surprise, then joy. She'd handed him the glove and tethers without hesitation.

"I had a raptor experience last summer," he said.

"With Pete. Yes, you told me."

"He showed me how to hold Clipper. A beautiful specimen. Back then, I was thinking of Daisy as if she were a new parishioner. I wanted to learn to attend to her."

Daisy stood tall and flexed her wings.

"She's thanking you," said Alison.

Matt adjusted his arm to help her balance, as he'd been taught to do. He gazed at Daisy in wonderment at her alert stance, at the gleam in her eye, at the lightness of her body so well adapted to flight and to the hunt. He thought again about Clipper, his beauty, his fullness of life. For a moment, he understood Alison's improbable professions of faith. She had once said "Daisy is a prayerful bird. I believe Daisy is capable of love."

Only now, it felt as if Daisy wanted him to speak.

"Life's a funny thing," he said. "I went to Vietnam and ended up on drugs. I had a rough youth, but I got help, and I found my calling."

"I didn't realize."

He knew that this young woman had never heard him speak about his life, no less troubled than her own had been.

"It's true. And I am so sorry, Alison, that I didn't reach out to you when you were in trouble," he said. "I of all people, should have noticed."

Alison gazed at Daisy's elegant form as if it would yield her reply. "Later you helped me," she said.

Matt was puzzled.

"You accepted Daisy. You let her come to Mass with me."

Matt fell silent. "May I bless her?" he said at last.

Alison said yes.

His hand brushed Daisy's head, the soft, tufted warmth of it. *"By the power of your love, enable her to live according to your plan."* As he prayed, Matt felt an ache of tenderness for the life of this creature so unlike himself. He wondered if God ached like this for love of all creation.

What Alison Didn't Tell Matt

KNOWING THAT ST. BART'S would soon close, Alison had been making the rounds of Catholic churches in Boston in order to find a parish where both she and Daisy would be comfortable. None of them would admit Daisy to Mass. In one instance, she made it past a distracted greeter in the vestibule, only to be reprimanded later by the celebrant, who had noticed Daisy's seventh-inning stretch during a lengthy Eucharistic prayer.

Alison tried for appointments with various pastors, but they had been warned by colleagues that a nutty Bird Lady wanted to bring a "hawk" to Mass with her, and that raptors were predators and hyper-defecators. All answered her request through emails citing parish policy toward pets and various diocesan restrictions on the admission of animals to Mass.

One assistant pastor, a doctoral student, referenced an obscure second-century Greek text, the *Physiologus*, which argued that among birds, only the pelican bore pride of place in Christian metaphor, shedding its blood for the life of its young. Injured falcons didn't count.

That was when Alison understood the gift that Matt had given her.

She shared her experiences with her birding/theology group. "Daisy is a prayerful bird," she insisted. They all agreed.

Remembering her father's words, she felt at peace. "Our

Creator burst the bonds of death. God cannot be confined to a building or a tomb."

Alison had no immediate plans to return to church. On Sundays, she sat in the Public Garden, where Daisy would give praise to God by lifting her wings to the sky.

The Torch

AFTER ALISON LEFT, MATT DECIDED to go walking. It had been a warm afternoon, but he felt the coolness of oncoming night and the consolation of darkness. On impulse, he decided to make his way to the sea. Marconi Beach wasn't far, perhaps not the best choice for an evening stroll. Yet among all the beaches on the ocean side of the Cape, it alone had stairs that descended the steep dunes, which allowed the weary visitor a chance to enjoy the seaside. He could rest at the bottom, then take a meditative walk along the shore. On his return, he could ascend the stairs as slowly as he liked, with no competition from young bathers encrusted with sand, all of them hoisting picnic coolers and umbrellas up the dune like a hermit-crab battalion on the move.

Going where, he wondered. *And in such a hurry.*

He remembered that he had been young once.

Sad, perhaps, that he no longer was.

Reaching the bottom of the stairs, he walked along the shore, pondering the conversation he'd had with his superior.

"You wanted to work with the homeless. Why?"

"I felt I was one of them. Weak and beholden to God."

"You were too weak, Matt. You developed a drinking problem.

"Yes." He paused. "I have no excuses. I place myself in God's hands."

"You are also a humble man," said his superior. "In your time here, you've come to see yourself as you are."

Matt did not mention Alison, the harm he'd done her by failing to act.

He walked on the beach, under the stars, remembering how it used to feel, the warmth that seized his limbs when he drank. It would take him over, breaking him down into his dissolute human parts, until he believed that he would crumble into dust, return to some primitive, particulate state of being, and having suffered the end of arrogance, he would be re-formed, made again of finer clay, thrown by the potter's hand, fired in the kiln, shaped into a pot with emptiness and silence at its core. He felt this happening now, a peculiar numbness, as if parts of his body were fading into sleep.

As he looked up to the sky, he saw the stars dissolve into smudges of brilliant light. A blur.

He could not remember where he was. How he had come to the sea.

Walking over to a dune, he was aware that the tide was coming in. He lowered himself to the ground, leaning into the sandy slope, the tangle of beach grass and goldenrod, and, closer now, the gentle *shush-shushing* of the waves.

Dizzy. It will pass.

He closed his eyes, and then he heard a man's voice. His superior was sitting beside him.

"There's more to your story," the man said.

"I have a parishioner who is fostering an injured peregrine falcon," Matt began. "The bird cannot fly. She sees it as a child of God, a delight. I used to think this woman was a flake. Now I believe that in this bird's silence, she hears the laughter of God."

The man looked at him. "And you've drawn this conclusion, how?"

"By spending time with the falcon. Birds have remarkable gifts. Ever since I missed that fatal flight, they have lifted me out of despondency. I have come to see that my parishioner has a special calling, to attend to the lowliest of God's creation."

"And what about you?" asked the man.

Matt closed his eyes, heard the prayer of Alison's father, heard the roaring of the sea inside his head.

"I am a transient being, homeless, and God is my shelter."

"I will lift up a falcon, a fiery torch to light the way home."

He said nothing. He could not articulate his thoughts.

He knew the words, but his tongue refused to speak.

Ruddy Turnstones

FATHER MATTHEW REILLY WAS FOUND DEAD, his body washed up on Marconi Beach, adjacent to Highway Six; the closest beach to Our Lady of Mercy Church at Shorehaven's south end. A coroner's inquest determined that he had suffered a stroke, that the incoming tide had taken away his body, then returned it to the shore.

"I saw him just that afternoon," said Alison. "He blessed Daisy. He wanted to hold her and then he asked if he could bless her." She spoke as if this deed should have protected him from death. She told this to Natalie, then to Elias, then to Father Ron who felt it would comfort her to have something to remember him by. He gave her the photo of Matt on his ordination day, his youthful face alight, and she brought it with her to the funeral Mass, placing it on his draped coffin.

The service took place at St. Bartholomew's Church in Boston. The funeral was its last major function before closing, and it attracted a large crowd of colleagues, parishioners, and friends. Cameron Byrne drove up from New York. Natalie and Elias joined Alison, who sat in a secluded corner so that fierce-looking Daisy would not distress mourners and first-time visitors to the parish. In his homily, Father Ron noted the breath of vision that Matt had brought to the parish, especially his acceptance of a parishioner's injured falcon, a creature that had won the hearts and inspired the faith of many younger congregants.

At the end of the service, Alison retrieved the photo of Father Matt, said goodbye to Cam, put Daisy back in her cage, and drove to Elias' and Natalie's home for lunch. Once having eaten, they'd planned to share stories and memories of Matt to relieve their sombre mood.

"Can't guarantee a lot of laughs," said Natalie. She joked about Matt's first blank look at the hawk poop on the church roof.

"We met on the plane to Toronto," said Elias. "He told me he'd gone birding with this 'woman theologian. Red hair.'"

Alison mentioned the catastrophic animal blessing on the feast of St. Francis.

"Daisy made a leap for the white mice. Then, I distracted her with a dead rat, and she shucked its little ears and toes all over the driveway. It was gross."

Natalie laughed. "I would've loved to have seen Matt's face."

"At least he didn't ban Daisy from the parish. He made friends with her."

Natalie paused. "He had an open mind, didn't he?"

She mentioned the Easter Sunday brunch when she and Elias announced their engagement, when she'd told Matt that she'd learned to cook from her Uncle James who was gay.

"Some priests are intolerant," she said. "But not Matt."

Alison agreed; she'd never known Matt to be doctrinaire. Yet her attention wandered as she found herself staring at a group of photos on the bookcase. She could not explain why she found them unnerving. One showed a young girl smiling at a red-haired man.

"Is that you?" she asked Natalie.

"Taken while Uncle James was teaching me how to make crêpes."

"And next to it? Who's that?"

"That's my uncle with his partner, Andre."

Something shivered at the back of Alison's neck, the breath of an unknown creature pushing its way through the sod of darkness and into the light of the known, the understood. She scrutinized the photo of the two men, then reached into her backpack, pulled out the framed photo of Father Matt and set it alongside the picture.

"What do you see?" she asked

Natalie gazed at it in silence. "Andre looks like Father Matt," she said at last. "Same expression."

"Andre's his double," said Alison.

"Andre had a famous dad," said Natalie. "He was adopted by a guy named Gerard Lefèvre. He's a French TV host in Canada. Andre's mom was pregnant before she got married, but her boyfriend ran off to Vietnam, and she fell in love on the rebound. Poor Gerard and Valerie. They still miss their son."

His son is asking to be recognized. He's here with us. Lefèvre. Andre Lefèvre.

Alison hesitated. "Maybe it's none of my business," she began. "But did Andre die on 9/11?"

"Yes," said Natalie. "And my uncle, too."

Alison showed them the prayer card that had slipped out under the door of Matt's office. "Read what's on the other side," she said.

In Loving Memory of Andre J. Lefèvre
18 February 1971 – 11 September 2001

"This card was Father Matt's," she said.

The room was silent. Alison imagined them as birds, ruddy turnstones by the shore, flipping over shells in search of a clam, a mussel, a creature to digest. In a moment, their minds had become a single, delicate organism, incessant in its movements, turning thoughts over, prying them loose from the hard shells of all that they could not imagine.

Elias remembered that first flight to Toronto, how he'd glanced over at Matt reading his breviary, how he saw the card then, how he glimpsed the name *Andre* before Matt's abrupt gesture hid it away.

Until now, he was the only one who'd seen it.

"He told me he went to Vietnam," said Alison.

Everyone stared at the photo of young Andre, who looked like Matt.

"He told me on the day he died," she said. "He asked if he could hold Daisy, and then he told me."

Silence.

"Poor Matt kept his secret," said Elias.

"All those years," said Natalie.

The man who looked through me, thought Alison. She thought about Andre's mother, the woman Matt abandoned. She wondered how long it took her to forgive him.

"My mom told me that Andre was a good soul," said Natalie. "And how much those two men loved each other."

Alison felt the dead clay of fear that trapped her body, then relief as it began to crack. Father Matt died in a prison of loneliness. She would not make that same mistake.

She could hear Cam's voice. "In the end, we will be judged by love."

She took Daisy out of her cage. The peregrine falcon stood tall on her gloved fist, wings spread, as if she could imagine flying.

Epilogue

@AlisonPeregrine Fr. Matt Reilly blessed Daisy on the day he died. She was the last living creature that he touched. #PrayingWithYourFalcon.

Acknowledgements

My heartfelt thanks to Inanna Publications and my publisher Luciana Ricciutelli for her warmth and friendship and for her generous response to my work. Thanks also to Val Fullard for her elegant cover design, and to publicist and marketing manager, Renée Knapp.

Thank you, Irene Guilford and Brian Gibson for your thoughtful reading of early drafts that helped me give shape to this manuscript. And Brian — kind-hearted birder and friend of the natural world — thank you for sharing your knowledge and for helping to weave the tender nest where this novel was born and took flight.

A shout-out to Ontario's Wye Marsh Wildlife Centre for providing me with a wonderful opportunity to "walk the hawk" and get hands-on practice in the care and feeding of raptors. It was an inspiring and eye-opening adventure. Thank you for your hospitality.

For three years, I took part in a chat room (which I still occasionally visit) sponsored by New York University to promote a nesting pair of red-tailed hawks that had taken up residence on campus. With a webcam, it was my first close-up experience of nesting birds, and witnessing their life cycle from egg-laying to first flight was a life-changing experience. Many thanks to all participants for sharing your affection for the hawks, and especially to falconer John Blakeman for detailed answers to all questions about raptors.

The beautiful campus of St. Michael's College in the University of Toronto provided much inspiration for this novel. I'm a St. Mike's grad, and hopefully, some of the wisdom gleaned from studying theology in later years has found a home in the writing of this book. Thank you.

Photo: Jorjas Photography

Carole Giangrande is the award-winning author of ten books, including the novella *A Gardener on the Moon* (winner of the 2010 Ken Klonsky Award) and the novel *All That Is Solid Melts Into Air* (2018 Independent Publishers Gold Medal for Literary Fiction). *The Tender Birds* is her fourth novel. She's worked as a broadcast journalist for CBC Radio, and her fiction, poetry, articles and reviews have appeared in literary journals and in Canada's major newspapers. In her spare time, she loves birding with her partner Brian, photographing birds and trying to improve her French.